The Moon*beamers*

It's never easy when you're the new partner...

GARY SEEARY

Cover photo and design
Cover photo: Seagull Rock, Mentone captured by Chris J Mitchell @
chrisjmitchellphotography
Cover and book design: Luke Harris. Working Type Design @workingtype

This is a work of fiction. Characters, institutions and organisations mentioned in this
novel are either the product of the author's imagination or, if real, used fictitiously
without any intent to describe actual conduct.

First published in 2020 by Gary Seeary Books, Mentone, Victoria, 3194
ISBN: 9780648002840 (novel)
ISBN: 9780648002857 (e-book)
Copyright © Gary Seeary 2020

-GS-

Prepublication Data Service entry is available from the National Library of Australia.
http://catalogue.nla.gov.au

Typeset in Arno Pro.
Printed by Lightning Source, Boronia.
Editor: Deborah Seeary

The author and publisher have made every effort to contact copyright holders for
material in this book. Any person or organisation that may have been overlooked
should contact the publisher.

About the author

Gary Seeary was born in the town of Stawell in the Wimmera region of Victoria. He currently lives with his wife, Deborah, in the bayside area of Melbourne.

They have two adult children and six grandchildren.

With an eclectic love of Australian and foreign literature, Gary dedicated his first novel, *Sebastian Carmichael*, to the era between the wane of Great Depression and the Second World War.

For his second novel, *The Beautiful Journey*, Gary returned to the place of his youth; the Wimmera of the late 70s.

For his latest novel, Gary brings it home to the bayside area of Melbourne. *The Moonbeamers* is the result.

Also by Gary Seeary

For the Moonbeamers,
the Esther Williams and the March Flies

There's a space in the back of my mind where you used to be
Like ghosts round a maypole you dance through my memory
I went looking for answers but I found that my heart had declined
And the face in the mirror tells me I'm doin' fine

Chris Wilson

PART ONE:
BEACH

1

Friday, 27th December 1996. Evening

Here she comes clomping up the stairs. Why can't she walk around the house like a normal person does, or like her mum? Fiona always walks so lightly on her tiny feet, yet still with purpose.

Although, there is some comfort in knowing where Pixie is at any given moment.

Her brother, Zac, is a different kettle of fish, he's barely audible as he shuffles and mopes about — I wish he'd stomp occasionally.

No need to wonder what Pixie has in store for me this evening. It will have everything to do with the carry-on of last night.

Some things are best left in the realms of the unknown.

"Michael, are you in there?" Pixie called from the top of the stairs.

"I sure am," I replied from inside the master bedroom.

"Can I come in?" Pixie asked.

"Sure," I replied positively, although wishing she'd just go back downstairs to her friends.

I *was* relaxed up until then, leaning against two large pillows on top of the firm king-sized bed I had found myself privileged to share twelve months ago; although only on a permanent basis for the past two.

In boxer shorts, I was in the process of reading the screenplay that Pixie's mum and my lover, Fiona, had adopted from the well-known bestseller, *The Money Trail*.

I timed Pixie's stomping and placed the script over my boxers as she burst into the room.

"Hi," Pixie said quickly and then turned back to close the door.

With the door firmly shut on the throbbing techno music that had recently commenced at the far end of the house, Pixie walked over and stood in front of the bed in barely a thread of a royal blue evening dress, before planting the fists she had formed on the way, firmly on her slim hips.

"Do you want to join us, Michael?" Pixie asked in an off-handed manner.

I straightened up against the pillows and smiled back at her. Pixie continued.

"We're having a little party in the family room — dancing and stuff … You know." Pixie's eyes weren't meeting mine, so I wasn't convinced this was a genuine invitation.

"You know Lou, she's there. You like her. You said that the other day."

I said 'she's alright' the other day.

"Thanks, but I don't think so. I'm engrossed in your mum's script of *The Money Trail,* it's too good to put down. I'd like to finish it in one go if I could. It's much better than the book."

Pixie began to stare at the script over my boxers, which I preferred she didn't.

Eyes up, thanks.

"Yeah, the book was a crock of shit." Pixie said in her usual colourful manner, "I read it at school. Mum's really put a cracker up its arse — I love it."

Thankfully, Pixie's eyes then returned to my face.

"I agree. Only one thing — Too heavy on the violence." I stated.

"Come on, Michael, don't be such a pussy. Everyone loves violence," Pixie said as she pretended to stab someone with an invisible knife. "Except the people getting bashed or killed, that is."

Pixie then sat without asking at the end of the bed, below my feet. I gradually closed my legs.

"Are you going somewhere later?" I asked to make

conversation, feeling she wanted to say something. "You look dressed for a night out."

"I wish I was. I wanted to see if Lou and I could get into a club in the city, but she doesn't want to go. She wants to stay here with her juvenile friggin' friends." Pixie replied with a fair degree of annoyance.

"I'm over hanging around with those Sailing Club tossers. Might end up like Tracey."

Don't start on her.

Pixie pulled her long blonde hair into a ponytail and then let it go of it just as quickly. She preened its full length one time and then stopped.

"Why are you here, Michael? ... I mean, why are you still here? Mum's away and you're here. It's bullshit." Pixie said at me, and then seemed to search for preplanned words.

"Zac and I don't feel comfortable."

Well, that's a nice welcome into the fold — and Zac only knows comfortable.

Pixie stood, feigned a look of supremacy and then smoothed down her dress as if I was being rude for not giving an immediate answer.

"Bad luck," I said flatly. "Your mum and I worked it out before she left. She doesn't want any big parties. Besides, I live here, too."

Pixie walked back towards the door and then spun around to face me.

6

"You know, Dad's barely gone and you're acting like the boss around here. You could be a sick fucker for all we know — and we're stuck with you. Who knows what you were up to last night."

"I was checking out a noise."

"Were you … really?" Pixie asked, her eyes held wide open for emphasis. "Do you always perv on people when you're checking out a noise?"

"Would you like to talk about last night? I'm happy to." I asked seriously, confident it was the real reason she was here.

Pixie turned her face away dismissively, showing a lack of maturity on her behalf. I took another tack.

"Have you spoken to Zac?" I asked, although feeling she would have probably let that slide, seeing little sign of the closeness with her brother that would be required to discuss such a delicate subject.

"He's *my* brother, so what he does has nothing to do with you." Pixie replied, trying for bitterness, but ending up sounding like a child. She then whispered.

"I wish you'd give us some space."

"Like I said before — bad luck. And by the way, I've been trying not to disrupt your, or Zac's, day to day life by being here?"

"Have you…?"

Pixie walked back to the bed, her face still turned away so she didn't have to look me in the eye.

"I asked Mum why you got divorced. She said I should think about growing up pretty soon … but I still wouldn't mind knowing."

"No, that's fine. I've got nothing to hide."

I'm shutting this down, she's crossed a line by asking about something I would probably share with her in time.

How could I explain in this room, on this bed, which was still far from being mine, what brought an end to the wonderful life I had, with a wonderful woman? — I rushed my words.

"Okay, it's simple. We wanted different things. That's the whole story."

I placed the script on the bed, swung around to its edge and then leant down to pick up my denim shorts.

"Alright, I'd love to come down," I said through a forced smile. "Could be a blast."

Pixie couldn't wait to respond.

"Now, you're talking shit."

My feet got tangled as I tried to pull up my shorts in rapid time; giving up in frustration, I turned to face my inquisitor.

"What do you want from me, Pixie?"

Pixie waved a finger at me in a dismissive way as if she didn't need to justify her words, or should ever have to, and then wrapped her arms over her chest.

"I just want to know if you're serious about Mum," Pixie asked perhaps never believing I was.

"Okay, I'll call my folks tomorrow and ask if they're happy to have their grown-up son back with them for a few days, then I'll see you and Zac when your mum returns. I hope that's comfortable enough for you?"

Pixie stomped back towards the door, opened it fully and then without being courteous enough to turn around to face me, said.

"Weak as piss."

I wasn't going to engage anymore. It would only turn into a slanging match. I had given her what she wanted.

"Don't forget, you'll need to walk Horry every morning now," I added firmly.

Pixie continued to stand in the doorway with her back to me, then whispered. I could just make out her words.

"I miss my dad."

She left before I had time to say, 'I love your mum.'

~

2

The previous night...

You have the most kissable lips, Fiona Farnes.

In the middle of the night, with my hand planted squarely on my cheek, and with the aid of a thin shaft of streetlight that had managed to find a gap through heavy drapes, I studied Fiona's fine and pretty features.

She laid peacefully asleep on a black silk pillow; her mouth held open just wide enough to let out soft breath. *You are beautiful.*

Hang on, your teeth are quite big, though — Michael, stop this, you've got to find a way to get some sleep.

But, I couldn't. It was too hot in this upstairs room that had faced a relentless afternoon sun and too quiet on the resultant sultry evening. Few cars passed on Beach Road and the chatting of stragglers from the beach had long since faded into the night.

I shouldn't be surprised by this lack of activity. It

was the night after Boxing Day, and the majority of people had already left town or were done in after a big Christmas — Except for me.

I decided I might as well roll over and stare at the ceiling for a while, something may have changed in the last ten minutes. I shifted my weight and tried not to disturb Fiona who had to leave for Sydney early in the morning; the not so glamorous part of being a film producer.

Bloody American film executives. Can't you leave her alone until the New Year?

As I settled on my back and noticed again how well matched the light-fitting above the bed was to the room, I heard a thumping sound that appeared to emanate from the back of the house. It was a dull thud like something, or someone had hit a wooden object, perhaps a wooden fence; perhaps our wooden fence.

I turned to see if Fiona had noticed the sound, but her perfect lips stayed as perfectly open as they had a minute earlier. There was only one thing to do for a bump in the night. Get up and check it out. After all, I wasn't going to fall asleep at any time soon.

As gently and as quietly as possible I exited our bed, put on boxer shorts and then headed downstairs without turning on a light.

At the bottom of the stairs, I shuffled about and found the pair of sandals I leave under the small table in the foyer, for my convenience and to Fiona's annoyance.

As I slipped a foot into one of the sandals I noticed that the door to Zac's room, normally firmly shut, had been left centimetres open. Then, I heard a faint, muffled voice coming from the rear of the house. It sounded like Zac's. I had to assume he was like me unable to sleep and was probably in the backyard playing with Horace, the family's elderly golden retriever.

I then snuck past the barely ajar door to Pixie's room, able to hear her heavy breath as she slept, before moving quietly into the family room at the rear of the house where my eyes were drawn immediately to the small and only illumination; a clock radio on the kitchen bench. The display flopped over to two-forty five as I stepped past it on my way to venetian blinds at the far end of the room.

Through two slats that crimped and cracked as they opened, and with only the meagre glow from the moon at my disposal, I could just make out the backyard and pool area.

Close to the house was Horace, alone and lying prostrate, fast asleep on a carpet square outside his kennel. No other living form attracted my attention.

Horry would be disturbed if a stranger was in the back-yard, so Zac must be out there somewhere — but where?

Just in case there *was* something sinister going on, I decided to sneak out through the garage door, go quietly along the gravel path next to the vegetable garden, where I'd be hidden in the shadows on the far side of the house; to observe whoever, or whatever, was causing me to wander about in the middle of the night.

~

I had almost slipped on the gravel in my worn sandals before I settled myself against the warmth of the house render near the rear of the house and waited for my eyes to adjust. It didn't take long to find my prey.

Opposite to where I stood, and not concealed well enough by the shadow of the pool-house, a tall, thin figure in shorts with scruffy shoulder-length hair was being pressed against the outer wall of the pool-house. It had to be Zac.

Pressing him against the wall and then kissing him was a girl dressed in a short summer nightie; her distinctive large-chested silhouette and the bob of her hair gave her away as Tracey; Roz and Jerry's daughter from next door; the same girl who Fiona asked in for a swim on Christmas Eve.

Tracey and Zac swam together in the pool that night, but didn't approach each other, and only spoke as long time neighbours would — which they were — but *this* wasn't swimming and Tracey was three years older than Zac.

And he is only fifteen.

Tracey drew the top of Zac's shorts towards her, which must have been boxers because they stretched out easily, she peeked inside and then drew Zac closer to her. Zac grabbed the back of her legs below the nightie and then moved his hands higher until they covered her bare behind.

Okay! I think it's time I go.

However, I was concerned about their age difference, and what, if anything, I should do about it. All I knew was if I was going to do something, it had better be done soon, as Tracey had grabbed Zac's hand and was leading him inside the pool-house.

I contemplated and then shook my head.

No, it's not my place to interfere with Fiona's family. I'm going back inside.

Then, it was too late, Tracey slid the glass-panelled door shut and moved Zac to the base of the single bed where she pulled down his boxer shorts and then pushed him forcefully backwards onto the bed.

"What the fuck are you doing, Michael!"

Holy shit!

I almost jumped out of my skin as I spun around to see Pixie in silk pyjamas standing directly behind me.

"For Christ's sake, Pixie! You nearly scared the shit out of me." I managed to whisper, a thousand terrible scenarios arriving with her. "Can you please be quiet?"

"Why?" Pixie replied, not realising the gravity of the situation that we were now both in.

I indicated for Pixie to face the pool-house, only to see Tracey pull her hair back over her ears and then kneel at the base of the single bed.

"Is that Tracey?" Pixie asked a lot quieter and then studied closely the activity within the pool-house. "Who's lying on the bed? … Is it Zac?"

"I'm pretty sure it is," I replied, unlikely to believe it could be anyone else.

"Jesus!" Pixie said even quieter and then seemed to gather her thoughts before continuing on in a whisper.

"Michael, what are you doing out here? Are you perving on them?"

"No, I am not. I heard a noise coming from the back of the house and came down to check it out."

Pixie's attention turned again to the pool-house.

"Me. I smelt an over-sexed, middle-aged man sneak past my bedroom door. Bloody hell, Mum'd freak out if she caught all of us in the backyard together. Never mind what's goin' on in there."

Pixie stepped beside me.

"I'm not sure your mum needs to know about this." I continued as quietly as Pixie had, trying to suggest she didn't go blabbing, "But, there is a big age difference between them."

Pixie and I were speechless for a moment, contemplating the now frenetic activity at the end of the bed.

2

"She's good, isn't she?" Pixie said casually. "That takes me back."

I turned to look at Pixie, quite confused.

"What do you mean?"

"Umm…" Pixie hesitated as if unsure she should continue. "Trace licked my lolly when I was Zac's age. In the pool-house, as well."

What the hell?

"It wasn't the same, though, 'cause we're closer in age and different actions, of course."

I can't believe this…

Pixie turned to face me and then found a spot on a partially submerged sleeper in front of a lemon tree, to enlighten me further.

"I thought about telling Dad what happened. I don't think he would have gone ape-shit. Probably couldn't care less. He told me he'd tried a few things when he was younger. So, I let Tracey do it again a couple of weeks later."

A breeze picked up as Tracey's parents' air-conditioning unit rattled to life, and I was eternally thankful that their bedroom was on the other side of the house. Suddenly, I felt Pixie's shorts touch my legs as she rocked back and forth on the sleeper. I moved away and pressed myself against the render of the house. Unfortunately, Pixie wanted to say more.

"Trace told me to lay back and enjoy it. So, I did. I've thought about trying a bit of vag myself. I don't know how I'd go. A hot chick asked me to do it to her one night near Stinky Corner … but I chickened out."

"You could talk to your mum about these things." I stated without trying to preach, "I'm sure she'd understand."

"Nuh. Mum doesn't get me like Dad does."

Then go and tell him — Not me!

Again our eyes returned to the pool-house.

"You know, Tracey shouldn't be with Zac at all. He's a minor to her. She could get into a lot of trouble for this."

"I'm going to break them up … Discretely."

"Don't be a prick." Pixie said straight away and then placed her hand lightly on my shoulder before I could move. "My bro's just gettin' a little education. He'll be sixteen in a few weeks, anyway. It's good for Zac, give him some motivation."

"And you've got to admit, he's hanging on pretty well for a young fella." Pixie then squeezed my shoulder. "Could you hang on that long when you first got … head?"

Involuntarily, though fighting with all the power I could muster at this time in the morning, the end of my penis pushed out through the slit at the front of my boxers. There was only feeble moonlight reaching this area, so Pixie mightn't notice.

"I'm going inside, Pixie. See you in the morning." I said hastily and then turned away to leave while facing the house, before trying to move as quietly as possible along the gravel path that led back to the garage.

"Inside's the word." Pixie said smartly, "I know why Mum's more relaxed lately."

I stopped but didn't turn around completely.

"Okay, I'll leave it up to you what you tell your mum." I whispered, "But don't forget, Pix, she's leaving for Sydney early in the morning."

"You don't get to call me, Pix — Mickey." Pixie replied in a low sneer.

"Sorry, Patricia. I forgot my place."

With that, I disappeared quickly into the garage, snuck through it and then opened the door to the family room. A row of downlights came on as I entered.

Shit! I hope Fiona hasn't heard Pixie and I talking outside.

A second later, Fiona closed the door to the hallway and then stepped into the kitchen wearing the same Japanese patterned silk pyjamas as Pixie. She then faced me, oblivious to current events.

"There you are." Fiona whispered, looking fresh from her deep sleep, and then placed her hands on her hips, "I got a fright when you weren't in bed and I wanted to give a certain piece of you a lot of attention."

Fiona looked down and smiled at the bulge in my boxers and then began to rock back and forth as Pixie had outside. I looked anxiously at the garage door hoping like hell her daughter wasn't going to make an appearance; or her son and Tracey, for that matter.

"I heard a noise out the back." I explained, looking in the direction of the garden through the kitchen window, even though darkness filled the frame, "It sounded like something had hit the fence. Couldn't sleep, anyway, so I thought I'd check it out."

"Did it have long black brushy hair?"

"As a matter of fact, it did, Fee. I really get off on long black brushy hair." Fiona's eyes remained fixed on my boxers.

"I see that. That big bad brushy, or its rellies, have been hanging around here ever since we moved in. I'm glad you've finally got to meet one of them — Very glad."

With her pointer, Fiona waved me over, which I responded to immediately. When I reached her she kissed me passionately and then pulled me tightly against her warm body.

"Let's leave the brushy to eat our veggies. I need a memory to take to Sydney."

Fiona grabbed my hand and led me upstairs.

~

At the end of our king-size bed, I had no desire for fore-play. I pulled down Fiona's pyjama shorts and then pushed her backwards onto the black silk sheets below, shortly afterwards forcing my head between her thighs, desperate to taste the warmth and passion that awaited me there. Her aroma sent an urgency through my body that I could not contain.

I worked my arm under her spine and then with an irrepressible force lifted and turned her over in one motion. Without giving Fiona time, I entered her roughly almost brutally from behind. I had lost myself in the moment, I had forgotten who I was making love to. An image confronted me and I couldn't accept who it was or admit how much I wished it was her below me.

I continued to push harder and deeper inside Fiona until she leant back and touched my side. I ignored her. I didn't want to stop until I could rid myself of the unrelenting ache in my body and the tension that filled my mind.

Then realising the hurt and confusion I would be causing, I willed myself to stop.

"Whoa, cowboy!" Fiona said in a tone that questioned my actions. We then gently but awkwardly released from each other. I sat at her side, out of breath, then laid back on the coolness of the silk.

"Are you okay, Michael?" Fiona asked, after lying herself beside me, her face close to mine.

"Sorry, Fee, I got carried away. I'm sorry."

Fiona waited until my heart and breathing had calmed, then helped me up. She kissed me gently before slowly undoing her pyjama top and revealing her petite breasts, pale against the dark silk. She then slipped under the top sheet and held it open.

"Now, naughty boy. A little slower, please."

~

3

"Buh-boom! Exactly on time."

I didn't expect to hear those words only a second after entering the kitchen or to see Pixie standing in front of stove burners wearing an apron over her marine striped tank-top and frayed hot-pink shorts while whisking eggs in a bowl.

Seconds later, happy with the consistency, she poured the mixture carefully into a hot pan.

"Morning, Pixie," I said more cheerfully and politely than she deserved after her visit to my room last evening,

"Exactly on time for what?"

"Brekky." Pixie replied brightly and then returned to gently stir the scrambled eggs, before asking. "Are you hungry?"

"I am a bit," I replied, not as brightly as Pixie had asked, but she shouldn't be surprised. I had little sleep overnight because of the way our conversation had ended.

That conversation made me wonder if there was anything I could ever do that would make me feel like a real part of this family. Or maybe I shouldn't be so self-absorbed and think about how devastating it must have been for its actual members — when it fell apart.

All I know is, I love Fiona and her children.

Pixie then said in a way that perhaps acknowledged she had been out of line last night. "Good, 'cause I'm making you scrambolli and a strong coffee."

After opening a cupboard she stretched up and then grabbed out two mugs.

"You're gonna need double-shots every morning when you start teaching those skanks at the Girls' Secondary in Feb." Pixie said smartly.

She placed the mugs beside a glass coffee plunger on the bench.

"I'm sure they're lovely girls, at the Girls'." I returned just as smartly, "Just like you, Pixie."

Pixie smirked and then said in a posh English accent.

"Only joking, sir. A lot of 'em are skanks, though."

Pixie pressed down hard with both hands on the full plunger while batting her eyelids at me with a *please forgive me* expression on her face.

"You're not going are you?" Pixie asked quietly and then pouted her bottom lip. "I was just annoyed last night with Lou for not wanting to go out. Turned out okay, though. I kissed one of the new guys to the club. He's a few months older than me — Phew for that!"

Pixie then looked down at the eggs as she pushed and played with them, before rattling off another unwarranted story.

"I let him play with my little boobs for a while. You should have seen how hard he went. He nearly poked a hole in his shorts — Argh! He wanted me to touch it, but I kept teasing his leg."

I sat unfazed at the breakfast bench and then thought. *Enough of this rubbish.*

"You know, you don't need to tell me *all* of your private things. It's not really any of my business. And to be quite honest, I hear the same stuff at school — every day."

That might shut your potty mouth.

Pixie as if not listening, pushed the scrambled eggs onto toast in the centre of a plate, repeated the performance on a second, before pouring coffee into the two mugs on the bench.

"It'd be nice to sit outside. Wouldn't it?'

No use sucking up to me now, Jezebel.

"Sure, but you'd better not leave it too late to walk Horace. It's heating up real quick." I replied.

I opened the back door for Pixie to take the breakfast plates outside and then went back to grab the coffee mugs. A dappled light filled the vine-covered courtyard as we sat on the near corner of the timber outdoor setting.

"You're gonna miss, Horry when you're away." Pixie said before taking a sip of her coffee. "He loves you and will be so unhappy."

"Or, you will be so unhappy when your mum gets back and I'm not here."

"No..."

"Yes!"

"I'm really sorry about last night. I'm serious. I don't want to be left without an excuse for Lou. She thinks it would be cool to have a huge pool party here. Her silly friends would just go — silly."

I had a large gulp of coffee and then some scrambled eggs while I thought about this. Pixie put on a sad face.

"Alright, I'll stay," I said, relenting only because I didn't want my folks to think that things weren't working out for me, again.

Maybe, they weren't?

Pixie sprung to her feet, jumped up and down clapping her hands and then opened out her arms like she was about to hug me, before stepping back; perhaps not wanting to betray the person she missed the most.

"Yay!" Pixie shouted as she sat down again to finish her breakfast. After having a sip of coffee she asked with malt covered lips.

"Please come and walk Horry with me."

"Doesn't Lou normally tag along when you walk Horry?"

"Not that often," Pixie said and then leant forward as if to tell me a secret.

"Never repeat this, Michael, or else I'll stab you in the eye with a stick. But I'm sick of hanging around with Lou and all the other kids from the Sailing Club. They're so ... the same. Lou needs to get away from them," Pixie then pointed a finger at her head. "They're dulling her brain."

Teenagers can be so bloody selfish!

"Don't ever think you're too good to have a good friend like Lou."

Pixie looked at me annoyed and then a second later looked like she was about to cry until Horace walked up and licked the side of her leg.

"Ooh!' Pixie said as she squirmed. "I thought it was Tracey."

I'll pay that. I gave Pixie a tiny smile. For all of her misgivings, she could be funny at times.

"Alright, let's go if we're going." She said before banging her empty coffee mug down hard on the table.

"Okay — but," I got in quickly, "you're picking up the poo. And don't forget we need to get back by ten. Your mum said she would try to call us around then."

With that Pixie ran off to get Horace's lead, and I sat wondering who was getting led around.

~

4

At the bottom of our street, and at the corner of Beach Road, Pixie yelled at Horace, and by default, me.

"Horry, Run! Come on — Run! Run!"

We waited for one last car straggling behind a procession of others to pass, before first-time walkers together, Pixie and I, crossed to the opposite side of the road. Shortly after crossing, we meandered down the old boat ramp towards the walking path and beach beyond.

The bay stretched out in front of us, bright blue under an azure sky; separated and distinguishable only by a thin line of wispy cloud which ran from Mt Martha to Table Rock Point.

The neighbourhood and beyond was up early to enjoy this view, and take in the cool freshness of the still morning air; knowing that a blustery wind from the north would soon be bringing with it stifling heat.

Joggers, walkers, pushbike riders, dogs, parents with

kids, all crammed the walking path or crisscrossed the sand, ensuring a slow walk.

I handed Horace's lead to a relieved Pixie and then took the waste bags from her. As we approached the bottom of the ramp, Tracey turned from the walking path and began to walk up towards us; she appeared a little surprised to see us together.

"How are you two going?" Tracey asked politely as we met.

"Good, thanks, Tracey." I replied seconds after Pixie didn't, "Nice morning at the moment."

"Sure is. It's gonna get hot later, though…" Tracey's voice slowed as Pixie turned her back on her and then said to me,

"See ya, Michael." before striding off towards the path with Horace in tow.

"We'll chat another time — Okay," I said to Tracey, obviously hurt by Pixie's snub. Tracey acknowledged my attempt at an apology on someone else's behalf but remained visibly upset as she left. I took off after Pixie.

What is going on with that girl? She didn't seem that disturbed when she saw Tracey and Zac together in the pool-house.

I caught up with Pixie not long after she turned onto the walking path.

"That was rude."

Pixie spun around and said, only short of yelling.

"What do you expect? She's got some sick kiddie fetish — Do you think that's right?"

I couldn't argue, in a way, but she also had to accept some responsibility for what had occurred. She stopped me when I wanted to interrupt what was taking place in the pool-house — And as for the other matter with her and Tracey — that *was* disconcerting. I could only put both incidents down to phases — teenager phases.

I have only six days left as a substitute parent until Fiona returns — Surely, I can survive that.

Pixie looked in the direction of the beach below the Sailing Club, I followed her gaze and could see Lou and other members of the club pulling down the sail of a Minnow pointed into shore.

"Go this way," Pixie ordered and then tugged on Horace's lead to make him walk away from the club.

"This way's a lot longer for Horry," I said and then waited for almost a minute while we steered our way through the throng using the footpath before Pixie responded with a question on her pet subject.

"What did you mean last night when you said you and your ex wanted different things?"

I was hoping you'd have let that go, Pixie.

"Just like I said, you can't know everything about your partner when you first get married. You shouldn't, anyway. But, maybe you should decide on the important things, beforehand."

I pointed out a flock of gannet, not far offshore, diving into a school of baitfish.

"How good is that?" I said, exaggerating interest. "Birds are so fascinating, don't you think?" No response was offered to my poor effort to try to change the subject.

If she really wants to know. I should tell her the truth.

"My ex, Liz, and I had a blast when we were first married," I said somewhat relieved to launch into my story,

"Parties, travel, sleeping in half the day, but from the start, we both talked about children. After six years I suggested we get started. At the time she asked if we could hold off a little longer; we *were* having a good time. She said, two more years and it would be done. Two years later and nothing had changed. She shut down any mention of kids, and would *never* talk about it. I was at my wit's end. I felt betrayed … I left."

"Oh, wow — Michael!" Pixie exclaimed and then grabbed her bottom lip between her teeth as she looked at me while we walked.

"So, you cut loose the love of your life, for not wanting children. Whoa, that's freaky." Pixie said and then shook her head.

"You wanted to know." I eventually replied.

We walked again in silence. Every so often Pixie shook her head.

"I hope you don't expect Mum…" Pixie began, but I put an end to the sentence before she crossed another line.

"Pixie, please."

A few seconds later she asked another personal question, this time with a lighter tone.

"How long ago did you split?"

"Three years, three months."

"You sure you let go?" Pixie said quietly, almost to herself, and then asked with a grin. "After you separated, did you and your ex ever get back together for a quick bang?"

"We did actually, for a while. Perhaps, we were trying to patch things up. It was nice to hold her again, although it hurt every time we had to leave, or things turned bitter if I tried to bring up the subject of kids again. She was a huge part of my life and will always hold a special place." I said and then genuinely had to change the subject, or I *would* become upset.

"Now, do you want to head back along the path, Horry's starting to breathe heavily?"

We stopped in the shadow of the barbeque shelter for Horace to have a drink from a metal bowl left there for that purpose.

"No, just a little further. Can we go up the path after Seagull Rock?" Pixie asked. I nodded in agreement knowing she didn't want to go near the Sailing Club this morning, then suggested we get a hurry on as it was becoming uncomfortable with the number of people pushing past us.

"You know, Lou and I snuck down to watch you old guys on Christmas Eve. When you were meant to be swimming, but instead were cuddling each other."

Pixie looked for a reaction.

"We weren't cuddling," I said with a light-hearted dismissal. "It was just like a footy team after you kick a goal. A team hug."

"If you say so." Pixie replied with a broad grin on her face.

"We went down because Lou wanted to check out your freestyle — stroke." Pixie then put on an American accent. "That girl is boy crazy at the moment." Then quickly returned to the local vernacular.

"She was impressed with your stroke, but I thought, that's a little ho-hum. Must be cold in."

"Very funny," I replied and then added. "Christmas Eve was a funny night, all 'round. I'd only met your mum's friends three or four times. I didn't think we'd end up so close and touchy-feely with each other."

"I was only trying to fit in," I stated to a girl who must be well aware of the antics of her parents' friends. She then added with a wink.

"Exactly what I told Lou."

~

Opposite Seagull Rock, Pixie asked another question.

"When was your last girlfriend, or boyfriend, before Mum?" And then said something under her breath that sounded like 'Jerry'.

We stopped after the rock, at the bottom of the zig-zagged path that would soon lead us up to Beach Road.

"Girlfriend, thanks." I said with feigned annoyance, "A year and a half ago, I had a short-lived thing with a fellow teacher from my old school, but she took a VP position in Kilsyth. Neither of us felt strongly enough to travel. So that was that."

Horace crouched to have a poo.

"I said no shitting, Horry," Pixie said as she patted his head, content in knowing that I had the waste bags in hand.

"He can never make it back home."

I cleaned up under the watchful eyes of every passer-by and then binned the bag.

"Geez, that stinks." I said as my stomach churned, "We need to gang up on your mum and get him off Pal. It never sits well with any dog."

~

Pixie and I allowed Horace plenty of time to walk up the path; negotiate a short bush track, cross a carpark, and then flop himself down across the road from St Bede's College.

We waited until a pack of cyclists sped past and then crossed the road at a point not far down from Mentone Parade and the Mentone Hotel. After a short walk, we reached the hotel; a stir of activity noticeable inside.

"Don't tell Mum," Pixie said as we stopped again to give Horace a rest opposite the double doors of the main entrance,

"But I snuck into the Edgy with Beth, a friend from school, on a Wednesday night about four months ago. Beth's brother, who's a real nerd, made some fake ID's for us. He wanted me to give him something for it … Anyway, Beth and I lined up around the corner, we were sure we were gonna get sprung."

"Were you sprung?" I asked, although not concerned either way.

"No…" Pixie assured emphatically. "When we got inside, Beth and I went upstairs and started talking to these hot guys, except the more pissed Beth got, the more embarrassing she became. There's nothing worse than watching your friends get pissed when you can't. Hang on, didn't you and Mum meet at the Edgy?"

"We did," I replied. Pixie then looked again at the entrance, which would soon be opened and said nonchalantly.

"Okay, let's go."

~

"Your mum told me a while back you get a bad reaction from alcohol. Not that you'd be alone in that." I professed as we meandered further along Beach Road, "But, it is rare to be allergic to it. At least you miss out on getting sick at parties, or having a hangover the next day."

"Yeah, I guess. I do feel out of things sometimes with other kids. I can't even have one swig before I get all dizzy and my throat blows up like a pelican."

"Or a frigate bird," I added.

"Whatever..."

Pixie and I continued chatting happily until we got to the Girls' Grammar. I thought about it for a second, then asked anyway; she doesn't mind asking me curly questions.

"Have you got any plans for after school? It'll come around soon enough."

I gave Pixie a little time to ponder, then without a response, I inquired again.

"Is there any course you'd like to do at uni? If not, have you ever thought about stepping into the film limelight with your mum?"

Pixie turned her head sharply with a furious expression on her face.

"Limelight! You're bullshitting me, aren't you? The film industry is so boring, it's not funny." Pixie increased her pace. I kept up. Horace struggled. She kept talking.

"When Mum was filming *The Desert Crossing*, I stayed on set with her for two weeks. We were stuck out in the middle of South Australia somewhere. I was probably being a pain, but I was bored stiff. The crew were fun, even if I kept getting in their way. Mum was out there for three months."

Pixie then stopped dead in her tracks and swung around fully to face me, saying with bitterness.

"When she should have been *here* with me, Zac, and Dad. If Mum wasn't so obsessed with making stupid films — None of this would have happened.

Should I feel hurt?

Without any recognition that it may not have had anything to do with films, Pixie pulled hard on Horace's collar to make him reluctantly follow her quickly along the footpath.

I caught up to Pixie and Horace as they approached the Glen Court flats, which also formed the corner of our street. Pixie then said with a determination that forced me to listen.

"I want to tell you something that might surprise you — a lot."

"Okay, I'm all ears."

"You know how Mum and Dad split a year and a half ago."

"I was told so." I acknowledged while nodding my head, "It was well before I came along. Your mum did say the wind was blowing a gale here that winter."

"You mightn't believe this, but they never fought before they split. Don't you think that's weird? Surely people that don't get on — fight. And they were still screwing, even the night before Dad left. I could hear them — Eek!"

"They can't be over each other."

Pixie, Horace and I then stopped beside a massive aloe vera hedge on the far side of the flats. I wasn't happy.

"If your story was meant to get a reaction, Pixie. Well done — Great job."

"Your parent's separation kills you, I get it. But, I *don't* want to hear about it anymore and I'm *not* going to wear it."

I walked quickly up Naples Road. Pixie crouched down and buried her face in Horace's fur.

~

.

5

"We're early." Doug, my off-sider in the Science Department said as he walked in front of me holding hands with his also teacher girlfriend, Stephanie. We followed the footpath as it curved to the right around the steps of an earlier entrance, and below the imposing tower that dominated the façade of the Mentone Hotel.

"Not by that much," I replied, breathing heavier than I should after only a short walk in the sun from Mentone Station,

"'Bout twenty minutes, or so. That's alright, call us the advance party."

"We might be the party," Doug said with more than a hint of sarcasm. "With so many pulling out."

"I always liked The Grand." Stephanie declared as she and Doug stepped off the Beach Road footpath to let a group of present carrying couples move past them and then step onto the tessellated tiles that led to the double-doored entrance to the hotel. "Everyone knows where it is."

"Yeah, in the main street of Frankston. We know 'cause we're from Frankston High," Doug said, exaggerating his point.

"Okay, Doug, I know it's a little out of our zone. But it doesn't hurt to have a change after nine years at the same joint."

An enormous bouncer of Islander descent pushed on a large glass handle to open the right side of the entrance double doors and then gave a small wave with his huge spare hand for us to come in.

"We better do as he says, we may need him to separate us from the locals later on," I said half-jokingly, before being moved forward with the help of an on-shore breeze that pushed through ti-trees above the beach. Stephanie pulled Doug by the arm in the direction of the entrance and then said through a smile, but with little jest.

"Come on, Dougie … A girl's not a camel."

~

Less than three seconds after entering the foyer, and with my eyes adjusting to the lack of bright sunlight. I noticed her.

Hello! Why haven't I come to the Mentone for a drink before?

In a roped-off area to the right of the entrance foyer where I stood with Doug, Stephanie already lined up at the bar to get us a drink, sat a lady on the far side of a high table in animated conversation with a group of six or seven people around my age: middle. Her broad smile and brilliant blue eyes lit up the area where she sat. I kept looking, I couldn't help but look.

Doug grabbed my arm, distracting my attention from the woman I *must* get to know.

"Hey, that's our area, isn't it?"

I searched around and saw standing at the front of the cordoned-off area where the lady and her group sat, a metal-framed sign that read:

Reserved area:

Frankston High School Xmas Break-up.

"Can't they read around here, Michael?" Doug asked, and then looked for someone in authority so he could complain to them about the interlopers in our reserve.

"Don't forget we're early. The show doesn't officially kick off until six-thirty." I said steadily becoming irritated by Doug's negative attitude.

Doug pointed out a well-groomed man in pleated black pants, stiff white shirt and emerald green tie, standing beside and directing staff from a lectern at the opening to the bistro section.

Again my eyes returned to the lady at the same time as she placed her left hand over the right hand of a tall, almost too thin man, seated beside her. Immediately a thought sprang to mind.

Damn! I hope they're not an item — or married.

"Michael, come with me, I'm gonna find out what's going on around this place. The bloke out front of the bistro seems to know what he's on about." Doug said and then headed in his direction. I didn't want to, but I followed.

~

"Don't be concerned, I know them well." Said the man who introduced himself as Richard. "That's Jerry's group and they've promised to move on at exactly six-thirty. Which is..." Richard then checked his watch. "Twelve minutes from now."

Richard's attention was then distracted by a large group approaching the bistro entrance.

"Well then ... We'd better catch Stephanie before she waltzes into someone *else's* area with our drinks," Doug said loudly for emphasis and then returned to Richard, who he grudgingly asked,

"Can you get food in the main bar, like canapes?"

"We have bar snacks. We find them more appropriate." Richard returned sharply.

Getting a man off-side, let alone one who appears to be a professional and a gentleman to boot is not a good start to the evening. What I selfishly wanted though, was for the lady in our area to stay close by, so I could work out a way to introduce myself at some stage during the evening.

"Look, the group at the table could probably stay. It looks packed everywhere else." I declared abruptly. Doug looked at me confused and couldn't wait to say.

"Michael, what are you doing? You can't make that decision."

"Doug, we've had a lot more cancellations than the number of people seated at that table." I then directed my conversation to Richard.

"Quite a few of our troops have decided it's too far from Frankston to Mentone. The area will look empty with the numbers we're predicting."

Richard pondered for a few seconds.

"If you're comfortable sharing your area it makes my job of keeping everyone happy a lot easier," he stated. "And I can guarantee that every one of your group yet to arrive will be seated comfortably. I will also introduce you to Jerry's group when I get a chance."

"Would that suffice?"

Doug and I looked at each other and had no other choice than to nod our approval.

"That's great," I replied to Richard.

"Fine." Richard declared. "Now, I must attend to this large group."

~

"Hello, everyone. Happy forty-fifth birthday, Jerry." Richard declared with a smile as we approached those gathered around the table to celebrate it; Stephanie, Doug, and I remained a step behind,

"You don't look at all like you're halfway to ninety."

"Thanks, Richard. How kind of you to say that." Jerry acknowledged with a broad grin above his large bony jaw, while at the same time looking warily at our trio and then added.

"I have a feeling you have bad news for us, Richard."

"Well, you see," Richard said. "The cords that reach from one pole to the next, mean that an area is cordoned off. Usually for a legitimate reason."

"Is that what they're there for?" A large, rough-around-the-edges bloke said in a deep voice, as he looked around the table before patting Jerry on the back.

"For that exactly, Trev." Richard continued. "A party of teachers will be passing through those poles in approximately five minutes. And you know what teachers are like when they get stuck into it."

Everyone at the table realised something was up, and they hoped it involved them staying put.

"Richard, we're just like Richard Gere in *An Officer and a Gentleman* 'We got nowhere else to go!'" My hopefully future girlfriend said as she placed her hands together as if to pray.

"You sound like a movie buff," I said when no-one expected me to. Silence fell over the table, much to my dismay. My lady's eyes dilated from deep blue to a dull grey as she looked at me with a mixture of perplexity and wariness.

"You could say that." Jerry blurted out, which released a roll of laughter from her friends. I remained bewildered.

"Well, I have some good news for everyone." Richard declared. "These three generous people, Stephanie, Doug, and Michael, have graciously agreed to allow your good selves to stay at this table for the evening."

A chorus of thanks went up before Richard began to introduce us one by one to the grateful inhabitants. My anticipation grew as I moved closer to the woman I had in a short time become obsessed with. I finally shook her warm and soft hand as she spoke words that I failed to take in.

The best I could come up with was 'Hello'.

~

As I was lined up to buy more drinks, I caught out of the corner of my eye, a glimpse of the lady who I finally remembered was called Fiona, step between elaborate pillars at the entrance to the bar area. She shuffled behind a mass of drinkers and then was lost from my sight below the steps of the grand staircase that formed the centrepiece of the Mentone Hotel.

Seconds later, I smelt the subtle but distinctive scent of Anaïs Anaïs, noticeable on her at the table.

Fiona must be in line behind me.

I didn't want to be obvious and turn my head to make certain. I didn't want to appear desperate — I wasn't desperate. But I did want to feel again what it was like to desperately want someone.

"Thanks for letting us steal your table." Her soft voice whispered close to my ear. My body tensed. *It was her. I've got to say something. Something clever.* She spoke first.

"We would have had to pull the pin by now and leave if you hadn't let us stay. Standing up all night lost its appeal a few years back." Fiona declared with an almost youthful tone to her voice.

With my neck twisted back at an almost ninety-degree angle, I replied.

"I know the feeling. And don't worry, the table is no skin from my nose." I said and then cringed after giving such a lame and stupid response. I had to deliver better.

"Keeps our mob from breaking into cliquey groups." I finally got out. "No fun in that."

I turned back again to the bar and the line-up in front

of me: two unkempt barflies, one just-finished-work tradie and two young ladies dressed for a big night out; all waiting for the young and inexperienced on the other side of the polished wood to get their collective bartending act together.

And what am I doing about getting my arse into gear? I have a stunning woman within arm's reach. I have to make sure it stays that way.

I spun around one eighty degrees to face Fiona. "How rude! Turning my back on a beautiful lady."

Bloody hell! Did I say, beautiful lady? — You're an idiot, Michael.

Fiona looked from side to side as a trapped animal might do, if they were urgently seeking the nearest escape route.

"Sorry, can I start again? My name is Michael Freeman and as you may have guessed, a teacher from Frankston High. A biology teacher, in fact."

Fiona stuck out her hand, which I shook again with the help of a mild quiver in my arm.

"Pleased to meet you properly, Michael. You don't look like any biology teacher I had in school. Well actually, you sort of do, from the bird poop on your left shoulder."

I immediately contorted my head to the left to see a small white blob that had landed neatly on a small white patch at the top of my black and white check shirt. I cleaned the spot quickly with my handkerchief.

"How embarrassing," I said, now feeling more like a school kid than a teacher. "A pigeon must have got me on the way in."

"Or a seagull," Fiona added and then smiled effortlessly before continuing.

"Okay, I should introduce myself again. I'm Fiona, a local, and not found as often as I'd like at the Edgy. You know, work, kids, etcetera. But at least I've managed to make it down this evening for Jerry's birthday."

I looked quickly back to the line-up to check my position, which now consisted of only a squat, heavily tattooed man who must have pushed himself in while my attention was diverted.

"I'm not surprised you come here as often as you can. I love the feel of this place. Great architecture everywhere." I said with a renewed confidence which had arrived just in time.

"The skylight above us is amazing."

Fiona and I both looked straight up at the skylight, studied the bright colours of the lead-lighting, and then lowered our faces at exactly the same time; our eyes locked on each other.

"That hurts your neck," I mentioned for little reason, then looked for too long at Fiona's lips, which slowly tightened.

"Do you know what?" Fiona stated. "I've never noticed the skylight before," Her hands now on her hips. "In all the years I've been coming down here. Can you believe that?"

I looked quickly up again at the skylight and then returned to Fiona's incredible blue eyes.

"I can. I've missed the obvious before."

Fiona pointed to the bar. The tattooed man was gone. I was up. Then, before I could order.

"If you're after beer, the best value is the ten-dollar jugs and Richard asked us only a quarter of an hour ago if we wanted a bottle of Rosé that the bar staff had doubled-up on. You'll get it for bugger-all."

I hesitated before replying, simply because I had an overwhelming desire to forget the drinks and the Christmas break-up and everything else, and just kiss her right there and then.

"Great! Thanks for the heads up." I eventually replied.

"My pleasure." Fiona acknowledged and then added in a soft, sweet voice. "Another thing I can guarantee. There's a great view of the bay from upstairs, and we have plenty of time to catch the sunset. Trust me."

Out of the corner of my eye, I could see a young barman look daggers at me with impatience.

"I do. I'll see you up there in about fifteen."

Fiona gave one discrete nod of her head and that was all I needed.

~

I returned to my co-workers with a bargain bottle of rosé and a jug of draught and asked if anyone wanted to play a few rounds of Buck Hunter; I knew there would be no takers. I was free.

~

I was pleased with myself when I scored a respectable four hundred and seventy-five, first up for years, while also planning how to get upstairs without any of my compatriots asking if they could join me to check out the Edgy Bar.

I had waited my fifteen minutes, I couldn't wait any longer. I couldn't risk losing what wasn't mine — quite yet.

~

I found Fiona at the far end of the balcony window look-ing out onto a deep orange sky; streaky silver and purple clouds pushing across the horizon. Fiona moved her head and stretched her slim neck to look past a pillar, then noticed me watching her.

"Quick, quick, you've almost missed the sunset," Fiona shouted as she stood on tip-toes to get a better view. "Come here, the sky is incredible. Bloody hell, if they'd only let us out onto the balcony."

I stood behind Fiona easily catching the view from above her head. She touched my arm before pointing out a large cloud that had turned violet within seconds; pressed against me as she strove to see the final descent of the blood-red sun; more comfortable being close to me than I could have ever hoped for.

"The sunsets are magic this time of year. Just sensational." Fiona said, and then to my surprise, grabbed my arm above the wrist and dragged me across to the top of the stairwell and over to its far balustrading.

"Look down, you can see the whole bar area from here and like me, people hardly ever look up."

I searched our reserved area and could see my workmates dispersed into small groups. Fiona said she could pick out everyone seated around their table, except Jerry.

"Did you tell your friends you were coming up here?" Fiona asked in a whisper.

"No, I told them I was playing Buck Hunter," I replied just as quietly.

I faced Fiona and grabbed her left hand with my right. Without flinching, she held my gaze. Fiona then grabbed my left hand and indicated with a tilt of her head that she wanted me to follow her.

She led me behind a petition wall at the top of the staircase where we released hands. I seized her shoulders and then pushed her with restrained force against the plaster finish, kissing her with urgency seconds later;

our hips pressed firmly together. Instinctively, I took my hands from her shoulders and placed them unchallenged on her breasts, feeling firmness under my palms.

Fiona fumbled in her haste to lower the zipper of my jeans, succeeding only in jamming the fastener tight. Then with insistence, began to rub my groin until finally gripping it tightly. I inhaled.

"Have you got any plans?" Fiona asked through heavy breath, her lips close to mine.

"None that I can't change," I replied as I exhaled.

"Then, you have to come back to my house. There's some interesting wildlife there ... You're into biology, aren't you?"

"I am..."

A young couple took a peek behind the petition as they passed through to the residential end of the hotel and probably a vacant bed, giving us the thumbs up as they moved on. Fiona and I both laughed for a few seconds, perhaps from feeling again the exhilaration of first love; but this time without the angst of youth.

Fiona moved her hands up and found mine, placing them behind her waist. We then held each other tight.

Something good had begun and regardless of any obstacles in its path. I had to follow where it led.

~

6

Christmas Eve, 1996. Evening

I'm not hiding.

I was simply crouching in the swim-out at the far end
of Fiona's pool, taking in the character and mannerisms
of the people in the bubbling spa at the house end; who,
in truth, I hardly knew, or were sure how they fitted into
the grand scheme and hierarchy of this close-knit neighbourhood of Mentone; where I had found myself, simply
by the actions of meeting and then falling in love with a
beautiful woman.

Fiona said this was her real world, a place where the
pressures of her film industry career rarely intruded; a
world where she could be herself and feel safe with her
family and friends.

Nevertheless, I wanted for a few moments to step back,
or swim back, as was the case, to observe for a short time
what I might be in for.

I had been introduced briefly to Fiona's friends when we first met over a year ago, and then sporadically up until now — and I wasn't fooling myself — I was still the centre of attention.

Distracted from the spa, I followed the progress of a small bat as it skimmed in jagged patterns above the waterline hunting a meal from the abundance of insects swarming on this warm and still night. The bat then turned upwards before me, perhaps like Fiona's friends, unsure of what I was doing in their surrounds.

In the bubbling cauldron that was her spa, Fiona must have felt my eyes upon her, because she moved her head slightly from one side to the other as she chatted happily, touched her porcelain-white neck with unease while sitting between neighbours; Roz and Jerry, and Trev and Georgie.

From the moment I first set eyes on Fiona, I noticed a calm and presence about her when she engaged with others; which also included me. I was a lucky man to have been her lover for one year, two weeks and two days.

A very lucky man, indeed.

Then, Fiona's eyes were upon me. Seconds later, she left the raucous laughter of her friends and slipped over the rim of the circular spa as a crocodile would enter a waterhole. She proceeded to move through the water as smoothly and as silently as one would in hunting its prey. I could only anticipate.

"Hello, gorgeous man," Fiona said as she grabbed my shoulders.

"The spa dwellers think the creature from the black lagoon is spying upon them from back here." She then pressed down hard on my flesh forcing my head underwater. I surfaced and then saw through a stream of water, the bat return. It flew close over Fiona's head and again darted out of sight.

"Ooh!"

Fiona felt feverishly around the top of her head with wet hands; trickles of salt-chlorinated water running down her face.

"What was that, Michael? Is there a dragonfly in my hair?" Fiona asked and then shook with needless fear.

"I hate dragonflies."

"That my pretty lady was a Lesser Long-eared bat that buzzed your head," I said confidently as a biology teacher should, and then took Fiona's hands from her head and placed them together to try to calm her fidgeting.

"They're not common, not rare; and not afraid to eat dragonflies."

"That little fellow has been flying up and down the pool for the last half an hour — It saved me from a giant mosquito only minutes ago."

I let go of Fiona's hands and let mine slide down until they found the seam in her one-piece which ran vertically across the small of her back. I gripped her waist firmly and then pulled her towards me before gently kissing her cheek. She squirmed away.

"Stop that…" Fiona said pretending to complain in the way a teenage girl might.

"You know what I love — No! What I get excited by." Fiona said, returning to my arms. "Is a man who knows the technical name of a bat, who nearly gave the woman who loves him, a haircut on Christmas Eve?"

Fiona pushed me against the coping of the swim out and then kissed my lips so gently and softly that I barely felt her nails dig into my shoulders, deep enough to let me know she wanted me tonight.

"I'm gonna miss you so much next week, Michael. I hate those goddam Yankee film execs for separating us at this time of year," Fiona said, digging her nails in even further. "I can't believe I was silly enough to suggest they visit the Blue Mountains — I didn't mean with me. But it was too late. I should have suggested they had a break on their own, somewhere around Sydney Harbour."

"After all the film's set in Double Bay."

"I hate to say it, Fee, but you're gonna have to take one for the team on this," I said bending my arms back and then lifting my body onto the maroon coping of her pool.

"You told me this was the last hurdle to get your film over the line."

Fiona moved between my legs and her nails then found flesh on my lower back; her expression of annoyance at having to leave only made worse by the ripples of reflected pool light distorting her face.

"Bite the bullet and get it done," I emphasised, "Or else you'll be miserable right through till New Year."

"Argh! I could bloody scream. These blokes want a big name to lead, or they won't commit." Fiona said, restraining herself from shouting it out aloud. She then let go of me and slapped the water, only managing to again soak her frustrated face.

"I can't get the money for a foreign star. I don't want one, anyway. Barry Otto's on board, which is great, but I'm actually pushing for a young guy I saw audition for *Neighbours* to be the lead. They said he was overacting — Can you believe that? I thought he was brilliant and had perfect skin tone."

"You know, I went with these same guys to a baseball game in Chicago a few years back, when I was pushing my last film. Do you know what they asked me?"

"No, I can't even think what, Fee."

"They couldn't decide what they should eat during the game. They're Americans these guys — I thought, for fuck's sake, shove a friggin hotdog in ya gob!"

Thank goodness, Jerry, the most annoying by far of Fiona's friends, added a distraction.

He had taken his dripping wet body from the spa and then dragged it through the family room, where he had put on her favourite CD, *Live at the Continental*. After the first few bars of *You Will Surely Love Again*, Fiona's mind was distracted away from American movie executives.

Minutes later, Trev, who I was warming to as not a bad guy, let his over-the-top personality loose and stood as a good exhibitionist should, in the centre of the bubbling spa. Then pretending to be holding a mic, set about in a painful way, to distort the deep, soulful voice of Chris Wilson.

"I crawled cross the floor and chopped off just one more ... small line ... and the face in the mirror tells me — I'm doin' fine."

Jerry splashed about in the foaming circle as a roar went up from all other occupants, carrying on as if they'd never heard the song before. Fiona turned from me to sing and cheer as well. Chris was an obsession.

~

7

Out of the pool-house, Fiona's petite, and potentially problematic daughter, Pixie, strode, closely followed by her mostly fun but sometimes moody best friend, Lou. Seconds later, with their parents, Trev and Georgie, watching from the spa; Beau, a painful nine-year-old, and Isla, a reserved, just-turned-twelve-year-old, brought up the rear.

Stretched out like the Beatles crossing Abbey Road, the four marched in line and in time towards the swim-out where a more relaxed Fiona moved herself a discrete distance from me as if intimacy wasn't suitable for the young. Pixie reached the swim-out first.

"Mum. Beau and Isla are driving me and Lou crazy. They won't leave us alone for a second." Pixie whispered through gritted teeth as Lou reached her side.

"They're just kids, Pix. You were worse." Fiona replied quietly and without sympathy, "You used to stick to your older cousins like glue."

"Did not." Pixie said and then tapped Lou on the shoulder as Beau and Isla arrived.

"I think Beau and Isla are both gonna be taller than me and Pix," Lou said in an exaggerated manner to mask the true dialogue.

"Could be," Fiona replied. "The way they're shooting up at the moment." She then spoke to Isla.

"How are you, young lady? Getting excited about going to the Girls' Grammar next year?"

"I'll be fine, thanks, Mrs F," said the shy teen without feeling the need to elaborate.

"And what about you, Beau?" Fiona asked. "Still getting pains in your legs from all the growing up you're doing?"

Before Beau could answer, Pixie had trapped his arms and tried to push him towards the edge of the pool. Beau squirmed in an attempt to break free.

"Pix, don't be silly," Fiona said as she swam back in readiness to catch the struggling boy if he was thrown in. "You know Beau's terrified of the water."

"Stop, Pix. Please!" Beau yelled as he dropped to his knees. Pixie reluctantly let go.

"You live by the beach. You've got to learn to swim." Pixie yelled at Beau as he ran off towards his parents in the spa.

Pixie then mouthed to her mum and me. 'Got rid of one.' Before adding for all to hear and on a different subject.

"Mum, can we put on a different CD? We're sick of hearing this shit all the time."

"Language please, Pix. I suppose you want to put *Behind Closed Doors* on again. Personally, I'd prefer to listen to the Spice Girls than Charlie Rich." Fiona said as she wriggled back into my arms.

"Well, we wouldn't. The same as you won't stop playing Chris." Pixie replied sharply with a screwed up face.

"Alright, go and put it on then. If you must. But only once."

"Thanks, Mrs F," Lou said politely. Pixie, Lou, and their shadow, Isla, then strode off in a determined manner toward the family room. My major concern, apart from the water probably still lying on the polished floorboards, was how I would soon be the only adult left in this house when Fiona headed to Sydney.

"Fee, I've been thinking..." I said while trying to draw Fiona's attention away from the action at the house end of the pool.

"It might be better if I head off while you're away. I've only been staying here for a few months and I must seem like a stranger to Pixie and Zac. I can stay at my folks."

Fiona turned to me immediately. This subject must have been close to her thoughts.

"What do you mean? You met Pixie and Zac a year ago. You're making me angry by saying that. At some stage, they're going to have to get used to having you around."

"You are sticking around, aren't you?"

I answered without hesitation. "Of course I am, but..."

"No buts," Fiona said placing the palms of her hands flush with the surface of the water to somehow calm herself and then gave me a grin. "The primary relationship is between the adults. Too much pandering to what kids want, nowadays."

"You're making a lot of sense, Fee. I see kids playing their parents every day."

"There you go..." Fiona said and then she caught sight of two figures moving beneath the overgrown hedge at the side of her house.

"I think Steve and Jill are here."

I strained my eyes down the path. I could see the red tip of a cigarette swinging back and forth near the dull white glow of a polystyrene beer container. It had to be Steve, another neighbour, and a genuinely nice guy; a cigarette and Carlton Draught his constant companion.

Arriving with him was a contradiction to Steve's laid-back style: Jill, his wife; a woman who Fiona says lives a life of well-ordered discipline, mixed with the occasional over the top good time.

Steve burst out of the side path. "Hi, all. Got any spare ice in the Esky?" A 'Yeah' came from the spa a second later. Steve placed his small container down and then began grabbing cubes of ice from the larger.

7

Jill, after hesitating in the shadows, appeared in a Hawaiian Maxi dress while carrying a fruit flan.

"Well! Look who the cat's dragged in." Trev yelled as he exited the family room holding one green can on top of another.

"How ya doin' good neighbours? Hope ya brought ya togs."

"Already on, mate." Steve enthusiastically replied. "Jill couldn't find hers."

Jill went to step past Trev to take the flan into the kitchen. He stepped in front of her.

"Come on, Jill, you're talkin' to your mates, now. We know you love the water. I'm sure Fee's got a spare one piece lying around somewhere."

"Well, I don't feel like a swim at the moment, Trev. So don't pressure me. I swim when I want to."

"Okay, okay…" Trev accepted and let her pass, at the same time as Lou walked out of the double doors of the family room.

"Hi," Lou said, pleased to see her parents, and then added. "Where's my little bro. Doesn't he want to associate with us anymore?"

"Flynn's in bed, love. All tuckered out from the marker race this morning. You should have joined him." Steve said as he released white froth from the top of his white can.

"I couldn't," Lou said with annoyance. "Do you want to know why?" Her dad had a long sip of his beer, not interested in the reason. Then, Lou's eyes dilated and became fixed on the spa. I followed their trajectory.

"Mum! — What the hell are you doing?" she yelled.

Jill, who must have gone through the kitchen and then out the side door of the family room, took a step from the edge of the spa, into the middle; her loose Maxi dress ballooning out and covering the occupants surprised faces and evading bodies; the Maxi then sank as slowly as the seated came to realise what had just occurred.

"Well, you poked the bear, Trev," Jill said calmly while pulling her wet top away from a soaked black bra underneath.

Fiona laid back between my legs. "You'll get used to them."

"I dunno…" I said, but soon realised I shouldn't have.

Fiona moved away from me, a touch angry like before.

"Michael. These guys you don't know about … are my friends and they're bending their drooping arses over backwards to make you feel as welcome as possible — They could be pricks." Fiona then gave me a quick peck on the cheek.

"Come on. They're fun." Fiona swam off towards the spa and then stopped and turned back to me.

"And the blokes might even take you for a swim later."

I hesitated and then slowly swam towards the spa.

I don't think so.

~

8

I reached the spa and then leant my elbows on the rim. The din from the occupants quietened as they became aware of my presence. Trev, couldn't allow this lack of noise to continue for long.

"Hey, Michael. What's up?"

"Nothing much. Fiona just said you blokes might take me for a swim later." I gave a wink to Fiona. "What's that about?"

"Hop in, mate. We'll tell ya about our aquatic pursuits later." Trev said and then shuffled closer to the step of the spa and made his painfully shy wife, Georgie, do the same. I thought she was about to say something, but no, she didn't; which wasn't a problem, Trev would soon make up for it.

I slipped over the rim and worked myself into the spa, but couldn't manage to get away from Jerry, who squeezed in between his wife, Roz, and me. Fiona then moved Roz closer to her and immediately began chatting in-depth to her closest friend; a friend she often referred to as a confidant and rock in her life. I had to assume in part for support during the separation.

"Mickey, you've got no more beers left in the Esky," Jerry stated, the 'Mickey' part grating on my ears.

"Thanks for letting me know, Jerry — I've got more in the fridge down in the garage."

"We'll grab 'em." Pixie jumped in, who, unaware to me, was standing with Lou and Isla only a couple of metres from the spa. I wouldn't have thought it that interesting to listen to the *olds* crap on.

"You want the usual?" She asked in a matter of fact way.

"Yeah, reds thanks, Pixie. Grab half a dozen, if you don't mind — Actually, make it a dozen — Thanks, girls."

The three girls then ran off towards the garage. I closed my eyes and listened to *I Fell from a Great Height* and hoped I didn't have to talk to Jerry. Nevertheless, Jerry wanted to talk to me.

"Well, you've certainly put your dick in the till, Mickey boy," Jerry whispered too close to my ear. "Slipped it into a nice set up here. Big house, new school — instant family."

I nodded my head. *What else could I do — except hit the tosser?* I whispered in his ear.

"Yeah, I've done well. Had to put in the hard yards, though."

Thank God, the rest of Fiona's friends aren't pains in the butt like Jerry.

~

Over the side fence closest to the bay, a face appeared. The face of an attractive, late-teens girl. With mousy-blonde hair in a bob and a large white band drawing it off her face, she could have been an escapee from a Gidget movie. I had to assume it was Tracey, Jerry and Roz's daughter; she was in their backyard.

A cooler southerly breeze began to pick up as Tracey searched the backyard for a familiar face. She then saw her mum and dad in the spa and waved excitedly.

"Hi! — Hi, everyone. Merry Christmas!" and then as Tracey raised her right arm and waved it around, "Can you feel that? The Medic's starting to come in … This has been the hottest summer."

"It sure has, Trace, and a Merry Christmas to you, too," Fiona replied while turning sideways and resting her arm over Roz's shoulder.

"Would you like to come in for a swim?" Fiona asked. "The pools only got a slight green tinge to it."

I then remembered Fiona saying hello to Tracey a week or so back, as we crossed paths while walking the length of Mentone beach. She was strolling on her own that day, appearing deep in thought; a hint of loneliness noticeable.

From the side of the house that led to the garage, Pixie, Lou and Isla returned. The older girls carried six-packs of beer through their fingers and stopped immediately when they saw who was peering over the fence. Tracey noticed them as well and then said straight away.

"You know, I might come in for a swim. I'll come around the side."

Pixie and Lou with scowls on their faces reached the Esky close by the spa and then dropped the cans carelessly into the icy water; some of which splashed over my towel lying nearby; some ended up in the spa.

"Careful girls, you'll get us wet." Trev joked.

Fiona then gave Pixie a dirty look, which she tried to ignore.

"Can you go and hang Michael's towel up, please?" Fiona asked Pixie firmly.

Lou grabbed my towel and then touched Pixie on the shoulder. They both said 'Sorry', before storming off towards the pool-house with Isla in tow. Seconds later, Tracey appeared out of the overgrown path at the side of the house in a white bikini; heads turned accordingly.

"Have you been introduced to Trace, before?" Jerry asked as a whisper in my ear. I shook my head, a second later she was on the edge of the spa.

"Hi everyone," Tracey said and then looked down at me,

"Hang on, I know this guy," Tracey exclaimed and then took a second glance. "Didn't I see you walking with Mrs F, the other day?"

"You did and you might see me again," I replied as a person with a renewed enthusiasm for walking. "I'm getting a real love for the local beach."

"Why not, it's so different every day," Tracey added.

I moved to stand and offer Tracey my hand to shake, but Jerry grabbed my shoulder and held me down.

"Well, seeing you haven't been formally introduced, love. This is Fiona's new man, Michael. You know, out with the gnarly old plumber, in with the handsome teacher."

Roz then pushed her husband in the side.

"Don't listen to your dad, Trace. It's not all about looks … Although."

Roz gave me a flirtatious wave.

"Andy's good-looking, Dad, he just got a beer gut, that's all. That's what all you blokes are gonna get." Tracey declared with a cheeky grin and then leant down and offered me her hand, which I shook.

"Pleased to meet you, Michael. You're a lucky man to have met Mrs F. She's incredible."

"Enough of that, Trace," Fiona said a little embarrassed. "You need to go for a swim — Now."

"It's true," Tracey repeated louder as she straightened up and then strolled casually over to the edge of the pool, where she leant down and felt the water while staring coolly at Pixie and Lou inside the pool-house.

"The water's perfect, Mrs F."

With all eyes upon her, Tracey dove in. After surfacing

she turned to face the spa when perhaps she should have swum off.

"Dad nearly forgot. I need to bott some money, later on. Coles aren't giving me enough shifts."

~

Fiona and Roz were still in deep conversation; all others in the spa occupied, so unless I wanted Jerry to whisper in my ear all night, I needed to move onto some other topic. Reminiscing often works.

"You know, on a Friday, about a year and a couple of weeks ago," I stated clearly and sufficiently loud enough to grab everyone's attention. Trev put up his hand.

"Hang on, mate. I'm a tradie, I can't think that fast."

"Just over a year ago. I met Fiona." I said then blew her a kiss, and was pleased to hear a chorus of approval from the spa occupants.

"We know, Michael. We were there," Trev added, sending a spray of water over me.

"Happy birthday, by the way, Jerry, for two weeks back. Sorry I couldn't make your party." I said, without total honesty, the timing of my now former school's Christmas party again fortuitous.

"You know, it was only by chance that I ended up at the Edgy the night of your birthday celebration last year."

Jill put up her hand to halt proceedings.

8

"If this is going to be a long story, Michael, I'll need to top up my champagne. Trev, do the honours, please. I think Georgie wants some, too." I waited for this to be done, and then Jill got back to me.

"Carry on."

~

9

Tracey swam the perimeter of the pool like a cruising shark as I concluded my not exactly true to the letter story of what Fiona and I had got up to after we first met at the Mentone Hotel. Our fellow cohabitants in the spa respectfully kept the number of 'bullshit' or 'it never happened' comments to a minimum.

Jill then said while still picking her wet top away from her chest.

"So, after the Edgy, you met for a sneaky coffee to kick off your romance."

"There was nothing sneaky about it, Jill," Fiona said, feigning hurt. "Was there, Michael?"

I shook my head. "No, not at all."

Fiona then sat forward in the spa and whispered to all within.

"Andy and I were technically still married at the time,

although, as you may be aware," Her voice then took on a tinge of animosity. "He'd already moved in with his big-boobed Greek ho by then."

"That's it, Fee — Fire up!" Trev threw in and then just as quickly looked towards a figure that had just exited the rear doors of the family room.

Out of that room loped Fiona's teenage son, Zac, dressed in board shorts with a bright multi-coloured beach towel draped over his shoulder; while also wearing the dowdiness of having just woken from a long sleep. He turned his head as a surveillance camera might do towards the spa, then over to Pixie, Lou, and Isla in the pool-house, before finally finishing on Tracey, who continued to cruise the pool.

If *I couldn't care less* was an art form, Fiona's son was the grandmaster. And even though I saw a smidge of myself as a kid in him, and that of a multitude of other teens I have taught, his general slowness of movement and lack of interest in the world outside his room was excruciating.

"He's alive..." Steve yelled.

Zac's head turned slowly back to Steve in the spa.

"Oh, hi Steve ... Hi everyone else?"

A chorus of 'Hi, Zac!' and 'Merry Christmas, Zac!' returned from the spa.

"Hello, love. I was worried you weren't going to come out of your room till the New Year." Fiona said with a hint of sarcasm in her voice, although rarely concerned by her son's lack of drive.

"No, I thought it was about time I had a swim this summer."

Zac then turned and yelled to Tracey now swimming breaststroke around the pool.

"What's the water like, Trace?"

Tracey stopped swimming, stood up and then yelled back.

"Beautiful, Zach ... ery — Get in here!"

Out of the blue, Trev stood up and pulled his too-revealing Speedos even higher.

"Okay, you blokes, it's getting late, time for the big boys to have a swim in the big pool. Michael, better grab ya self a dry towel. I'll tell ya what our expedition's all about on the way to the beach." Trev then looked around the spa.

"Any of you girls wanna come down and watch our gear?"

Jill placed her hands over her eyes and then shook her head. "If you want us to watch your flabby arse gear — Then no way." Jill was then high-fived in turn by the female spa occupants.

My rear end was compared favourably to the others as I stepped out of the spa and walked over to the pool-house, before poking my head inside.

"Hi," I said to the three occupants inside. "Sorry to disturb."

On the single bed, Pixie and Lou were lying forward on their elbows painting Isla's toes. They rolled onto their backs as soon as they heard my voice.

"What can we do for you, Michael?" Pixie asked slowly. Lou couldn't hold back any longer and burst out laughing.

"Have you seen a green and blue beach towel in here?"

"I think Mum threw it in the cupboard during the week." Pixie replied. "I'll get it."

Pixie's eyes never left mine as she stepped over, leant down and then pulled out a faded blue and green towel from a weathered wooden cabinet, handing it to me with a grin on her face.

"You'd better be careful, Michael. I think your new mates have found some fresh meat to play with. All they're doing is letting out their hidden homo fantasies with these nudie swims — Especially, Jerry."

"Nudie swims?" I queried.

"Uh-huh!" Pixie continued. "If you feel something touch your butt, it may not be a flatty."

I saw Lou cover Isla's ears. "It could be a fatty."

The two older girls again cracked up laughing.

"How gross is it going to be, all those..." Lou started the sentence, but Pixie continued it.

"Old man's balls bobbing about in the surf, slapping into your..."

Pixie patted her behind before jumping back onto the

bed and wrestling Lou. Isla wriggled her head free and then ran out of the pool-house, telling the older girls to 'stop being idiots'.

"But maybe, this is your fantasy, Michael." Pixie stated as she sat up. "You met Mum so you could join Jerry and his bum-chums, and get into 'em — I think you did."

I shook my head as I went to leave, then decided to stop and give the girls something to think about.

"Maybe, I did…"

I left the pool-house to two giggling seventeen-year-old girls, who were nowhere near as mature as I would have expected.

~

10

Jerry ran down the old boat ramp excitedly, I hoped it wasn't because he wanted to get ahead of us, get his kit off in good time, and then greet us in all his glory when we arrived on the foreshore. Trev, Steve, and I walked casually, though also in good spirits towards the sand of a deserted Mentone Beach swept by a gentle breeze.

Trev turned to me as we approached the walking path.

"I hope you're not like Andy. Hung like a draught horse." he declared pointing to his right knee. "He used to give all of us the shits and a massive inadequacy complex with his long shlong. Greedy bastard."

"Don't worry, you're safe. I'll be crying shrinkage as soon as I hit cold water," I said in truth.

Steve surveyed up and down the shoreline. "It's low tide. We'll be running out a long way tonight before we hit cold water."

We stepped from the walking path onto the sand and could see with the help of the carpark light, an elongated shadow of Jerry as he lowered his lengthy board shorts to his ankles.

"Alright, so what's going on here?" I asked, mildly concerned for the first time in the evening. "Has your group got a name? Fiona mentioned something about moonbeams a while back."

"The Moonbeamers are who we are, and we're about nothing — really," Trev replied, sensing my unease. "If you feel like a swim in the bay, on any night, any time of the year, but usually at Christmas or New Year, doesn't matter, there's generally a Moonbeamer around who'll join you."

Then Steve threw in his explanation. "There's no rules, no presidents, no committees. You just have to have one swim in the bay with a Moonbeamer. Although, it's become common practice to have a wee drammy of Scotch beforehand. To warm the cockles."

"Okay," I accepted. "Sounds pretty laid back to me. Any of the Icebergers from around here in your intrepid group?"

Jerry responded as we reached his mottled nakedness. "They're the intrepid group. Getting up early, diving into freezing water. No, we're the anti ... the anti — the opposite. We swim when the water's warmer and we're half-tanked. More fun."

As if the minds of our quartet suddenly became synchronised, we searched up and down Mentone Beach to look for human activity. Obscured figures lying on the sand a hundred metres closer to Parkdale, may have been a couple making out.

Steve then concluded, "That's good, doesn't look like there's anybody nearby."

"We don't mind if there's the occasional adult wandering about having a gawk," Jerry added. "But we don't want to scare any kids."

No, we wouldn't want to get creepy — Would we, Jezz?

Trev flicked me with his towel and then said, "You look a little nervous, Michael. You know this is just an excuse for us guys to get away from the girls for a while and talk men things."

"What men things?" I asked.

Trev thought about it for a moment and then replied. "Women."

We found a spot closer to the water and then threw our towels into a pile.

Jerry threw his trunks and towel on top and then said, "I tell you now, working at the Casino has given me a real appreciation for the slender Asian form."

"Yeah, Jezz!" Trev exclaimed, "I've heard some of the Asian *girls* have nice figures, too."

Steve and I high-fived Trev before he rubbed Jerry on his bony head.

"You blokes aren't as funny as you think," Jerry complained, then quickly got over it and faced the small breaking waves.

"Alright, let's do this."

"Let the newbie lead the way," Trev said to Jerry and Steve, then turned to me,

"Michael, what you've got to do is run and keep running. Do *not* dive in until you're sure you've cleared the shallows. Or, you'll be eating a sand sandwich."

Trev dropped his Speedos, then Steve, his blue denim shorts. They all waited and watched as I dropped my new Billabong swimming trunks; Jerry looked for too long.

"I'm worried about you, Jezz." Trev declared and then asked. "Do you need to tell us something, mate?"

I didn't wait for the answer, only ran flat-out through warm shallows, standing on the occasional rock on the way. I took a peek behind and saw Steve and Trev next to each other; Jerry brought up the rear. I must have run thirty metres before I turned back and yelled.

"It can't be much further, can it?"

Steve and Trev waved me forward. I ran until I lost my footing and slipped into deep, cold water. In shock from the difference in temperature, my feet searched desperately for firm ground.

"Holy shit! It's bloody freezing here!" I yelled as I surfaced.

A few metres from me, Trev, Steve, and Jerry pulled up, laughing and yoo-hooing.

"Thanks, Michael," Trev shouted. "We're never sure where the cold water starts."

"You bastards," I shouted, spitting out saltwater, my feet finally managing to find firm sand. I worked my way back towards my pleased-with-themselves companions, as Trev added.

"You know, there was a report of a Hammerhead shark being spotted down this way, last week,"

"Bullshit!" Steve replied. "The hammerheads in the back of your ute are the only ones around here."

"It's not bullshit," Trev replied.

"Sharks are bottom and shore feeders," I added, thinking I could get a bit of my own back here. "The Parkdale reef used to be a breeding ground for Hammerheads, years ago … It's possible."

"We're meant to be scaring you, Michael. Not the other way around." Jerry shouted, not believing my story was true, just as a sizeable wave pushed his tall frame backwards. Then, when he regained his footing, he added.

"But of course, you're a bloody science teacher. You love sharks and shit like that."

"I don't like them that much. Especially, in their own backyard." I yelled back.

I began to shiver as the top of my body was exposed to the breeze the further I walked back into the shallows.

"What do we do now?" I asked, hoping warmth was involved.

"Well," Trev answered. "We go back to your house and you shout us a beer. Welcome to the Moonbeamers, Michael."

Trev, Steve and then Jerry, shook my hand before we turned towards the shore. Jerry then put his arms over Trev's shoulder and soon after mine. My back stiffened. Jerry looked over at Steve.

"Alright, Jezz," Steve relented. "I'll give you the full fantasy."

Steve put his arms over Trev and Jerry's shoulders, then we walked like a band of brothers towards the white lines of waves spreading on the shore. A second later I felt a light scrape against the back of my legs. Jerry must have felt it as well because he let out a yelp as he jumped high out of the water.

"Holy shit! I felt something on my leg." Jerry yelled, "What the hell was that?" His knobbly knees rising chest high.

"Don't know, mate. But I felt something too." Trev shrieked, as he began to push his barrel chest toward the sand as fast as he could.

"Let's get the fuck out of this water." He added.

Steve and I walked calmly as Trev and Jerry moved away from us; Trev's large quads and Jerry's massive feet splashing showers of water around them as they rose out of the shallows.

"Probably a large flathead," I said to an equally

unconcerned Steve. "If it was a White Pointer, it would have taken one of us without warning."

"Yeah, a small Banjo shark at worst," Steve concluded.

~

When we arrived back at the pool area via the side path, Fiona, Roz, Jill, and Georgie were still drinking and chatting happily in the spa. None of the kids, including Pixie, Lou, Tracey, or Zac, were to be seen.

"We have a brand new Moonbeamer," Trev shouted as he neared the spa, all the girls inside then stood and gave me an exaggerated cheer.

Fiona then asked with a broad grin on her face. "Were they gentle on you, Michael?"

"They respected my first time, Fee," I replied, rubbing my behind. "They said I'd get used to it."

As the chatter around the spa increased, I noticed Pixie open up and poke her head out of the right side of the double doors to the family room, and then said as if inconvenienced.

"' Bout time you got back."

Lou then stepped through the door holding hands with Isla, who looked like she was about to burst into tears; Beau followed in pyjamas, rubbing his sooky brown eyes.

"Mum, we went home and there weren't any presents

under the tree," Isla whined like a six-year-old, and then asked. "Has someone taken them?"

Beau then answered his sister. "Maybe, Santa didn't bring us any presents."

Trev looked at Georgie at the same time as Georgie looked at her husband.

"Bloody hell," Trev said discretely to Georgie. "I thought you wrapped the presents this afternoon."

"No." Georgie replied, speaking for the first time I could recall this evening, "You said we'd do it together before we went to bed."

"Shit!" Trev said to himself before turning to face his kids who were now both holding hands with Lou.

"Okay kids, Santa will be coming, but not while you're awake. So, Isla, Beau, get your skates on and grab your stuff. We got to go." Trev then looked back at Georgie.

"Santa's helpers have some work to do."

Georgie placed a towel over her shoulders and exited the spa before beginning to help Trev pick up their gear, which was strewn to all corners of the backyard.

The general consensus as a chill crept into the on-shore breeze, was that it was time to call it a night. Jill and Roz stepped out of the spa before Fiona, quickly wrapping their shivering bodies with large beach towels, before reaching down to pick up an assorted array of empty wine bottles, beer cans and rubbish, and placing them into empty beer cartons nearby.

As Fiona dried herself, she said. "Leave them, guys. Michael and I will clean this up."

"No, you won't, Fee, or Michael," Roz said, sweeping the pool area like a rampant seagull, shaming all others to do the same. Minutes later only a stack of three beer cartons filled with rubbish remained beside a bent over palm.

~

"If I don't see you tomorrow," Fiona said, kissing on the cheek one by one her departing friends while holding open the gate at the end of the side path. "Merry Christmas and have a great day."

Finally and while appearing done-in, Fiona waved goodbye to the last of her friends.

Fiona then wriggled her right hand into my left, kissed me on the cheek, and led me without a word spoken in the direction of the rear of the house and the silent backyard beyond.

~

11

New Year's Eve, 1996. Morning

Sunny morning, perfect temperature — This is not gonna last.

I observed the cloudless sky and the mood of the wind for the slightest sign of change. A gentle breeze barely moved the branches and fronds of the dozens of evergreens, ti-trees, pines, and palms in my beachside surroundings.

In faded denim shorts and worn sleeveless tee-shirt, I stood behind the open tailgate of my ageing Falcon station wagon and contemplated whether it was worth giving it a wash.

Dust and grit would be arriving within hours on a hot northerly wind, and as far as I could recall my car hadn't been washed so far this year; a little longer wouldn't hurt.

Instead, I picked up a pile of discarded rubbish from the back seat and gave the front compartment a good vacuum, hoping that my efforts would be sufficiently tiring to send me off into the deep sleep I have desperately searched for in the nine weeks since I moved in with Fiona.

Then the voice of my wife, my ex-wife, filled my thoughts, repeating the last words she had spoken to me before I moved out of our home.

'No matter how hard you try, Michael. You can never deceive yourself.'

Please, Liz — I'm not deceiving anyone — Let me go.

~

I received a strong whiff of myself and wished I had sprayed on more underarm deodorant as I dragged out from the tailgate an old piece of carpet. This poor excuse for a fitted mat had been shoved into position on more than one occasion to protect my belongings when I felt it time to move.

I held the piece of carpet in one hand while beating it with a garden stake held in the other over a strip of river rocks at the side of Fiona's drive. Across the road, a just as beaten up Land Rover pulled into Steve and Jill's driveway. Steve, Lou, Pixie and Flynn hopped out. Flynn, the rarely seen, sailing and fitness-obsessed son of Steve and Jill, carried a large sausage bag, probably full of yachting gear, into his home.

On his way inside, Steve saw me and waved in his usual friendly manner, then suddenly stopped and began to walk over the road towards me. Lou and Pixie followed behind.

"Michael, how are ya, mate?" Steve asked in an exaggerated way and with an equally excessive smile planted on his face as he arrived next to me at the tailgate.

I'm in for something here.

"...busy?" Steve asked.

"Not too bad," I replied, wishing he would just come out with what he wanted. "What's up?"

Steve then belatedly put his hand out for me to shake, at the same time as Pixie and Lou whispering to each other, reached the wagon.

"Feel like a drive?" Steve asked, and then re-planted the overstated smile on his face.

"Could do..." I replied, without any good reason to say no.

"I think us guys at the Sailing Club have underestimated how much work we've let ourselves in for by putting on such a big New Year's Eve show."

"What do you need?" I asked, throwing the garden stake to the side. "Because once this old piece of carpet goes in the back. I'm done."

With a solid shove, I pushed the carpet over the tailgate and snuggly back into its standard position on the tray of the wagon.

"Done!" I exclaimed.

"Great!" Steve said, but the signs of anxiety on his face weren't easing.

"We have one more load of balloons to pick up from Lombard's store in Moorabbin. Lou and Pix will give you a hand, the big bags are a little hard to handle on their own."

Pixie and Lou, continuing their childish behaviour, pretended to be squeezing something smaller, then giggled to each other.

"I'm not exactly sure where Lombard's is, mate. Might need an address," I asked.

"The girls will show you. I've gotta get back to the club. It's hit the fan back there."

Lou and Pixie helped themselves to the back seat, already annoying me with their constant need to whisper. I spoke to them through the window.

"You'll need to sit in the front on the way back. Okay?"

Steve tapped me on the shoulder to draw my attention, keen to head off towards the beach and the Sailing Club.

"Many thanks, mate." He said and then was gone.

~

My luck was in when I found a vacant car spot directly outside Lombard Party Supplies. I pulled my station wagon up sharply, happy to get out of it as soon as possible, so I didn't have to endure another second of Lou and Pixie's giggle-interrupted nonsense. I leant my head back in through the driver's side window and then said.

"I know it's hot and I haven't got air-conditioning, but I need you to wind up the windows almost to the top. I'll drop the backseat if you could go in and see what stage the order is up to. Thanks."

Lou and Pixie quickly wound up the windows, hopped out of the car and then ran inside after basically ignoring me for the entire trip. I shook my head and got on with the job.

~

I blinked several times as I entered Lombard's huge store, adjusting slowly to the difference between the fluorescent lighting inside and the brilliant sunlight outside.

Now, where the hell is Lou and Pixie? I asked them to do one simple thing.

To the left of the entrance, large bags full of multi-coloured balloons floated behind a timber counter, three deep with customers. At the end of that counter stood a young male assistant with black hair, lips, and nails, over his white-as-a-ghost face. He appeared beyond bored as he filled balloons from a tall gas cylinder.

Then, everybody in the store's attention was drawn to

Pixie and Lou as they squealed and jumped about while running towards me; both wearing feathered pirate hats and holding two large balloons against their chests.

"Michael!" Pixie shouted. "Do you think we'd look hot if our balloons were as big as these?"

Lou, who was normally more restrained than Pixie, then threw in her two-bob's worth. "I reckon we'd get lots and lots of boyfriends. Wooh!"

Pixie and Lou then rubbed their balloons against each other. Customers weren't sure what was going on, while staff seemed unimpressed by an exhibition they probably see on a regular basis.

"Okay girls — focus!" I said in such a way to let them know I was getting really pissed off. "What's happening with our order?"

"Geez," Pixie responded, dropping the balloons from her chest. "We're only having a bit of fun. No need to go all teacher on us."

Lou then answered my question in a more accepting way. "The goth is finishing the last bag now."

"Okay, sorry girls for getting all stroppy, but the temperature has probably gone up ten degrees outside since we got here. The sooner we get back and stash these balloons, the sooner we can all go for a swim."

~

Lou picked up my blue and green beach towel off the bench seat, stowed it between balloon bags in the back seat of the wagon and then slid over until her right leg touched my left as I sat ready to reverse out of the Lombard's parking bay. Pixie with her sour face on plonked herself down hard next to Lou. Not a second later, a balloon behind the front seat released its gas. The sound it produced started off as a low, vibrating purr, then increased into an excruciatingly long, high-pitched farting sound. All three occupants in the front seat went silent and with wincing eyes looked at each other.

"Was that you, Michael?" Pixie asked, a smirk replacing the scowl on her face, the girls resisting as hard as they could from bursting out with laughter. Pixie wound down her window.

"It wasn't me." I replied, keeping a straight face as I turned my head, "Must be you, Lou."

Lou immediately responded. "No, no, definitely Pix. She's the sneaky killer. No smell and then — Kapow!"

Pixie barely got out the words, 'No, it's you who needs the loo, Lou.' before completely cracking up, followed closely by Lou, and then finally me.

My wagon was as full of conversation as balloons during our drive down Warrigal Road to the Sailing Club.

~

12

The now happy trio of Pixie, Lou, and I carried the huge balloon bags down the carpark stairs on the right of the Sailing Club, and then inside the clubrooms.

I was stopped in my tracks after entering the main hall, struck by the transformation of a somewhat featureless room into what most people would imagine the deck of a pirate ship would look like; which would then, according to the theme advertised, be turned into a pirate party boat within hours.

Blocks, tackles, and stay ropes were overlaid with strings of lanterns, which also hung between and over masts, booms, jibs and sails suspended from the ceiling; all pointing in a roundabout way to the deck, also suitably decorated with orange lifesaving rings and webbed glass floats on its rails; a skull and cross-bones flag flew from a crow's nest above the bar.

Almost lost in the ship's nets and rigging on the right of the hall were four men setting up drums and mics on a small stand; a large sign behind them read, *XSESIVE*, the name of our courageous cover band for tonight's potentially stinking hot evening; Trev waved as he ran out a long electrical cord from the observer's room towards the bandstand to power the band's equipment.

Behind the drinks bar, Steve and Jill, the only friends of Fiona who were actual members of the Sailing Club, busied themselves stocking a fridge with beer, wine, and soft drinks.

I directed Pixie and Lou to tie the bags of balloons to two high and round tables in an area to the left of the bar, an area furthest away from open doors or the opening onto the deck. As they were doing this a tall teenage boy who had been helping a group of young club members stack chairs, walked up to them. He spoke to Pixie for a few seconds, who then leant her head forward and shook it several times, probably to make it clear to this young man that it was *no* to whatever he wanted.

Pixie grabbed Lou's arm and they walked briskly over to a group of girls eagerly watching the interaction.

This boy with a bad case of acne didn't seem to know what to do then, eventually walking slowly back with his head bowed in the direction of a small group of boys his own age; around seventeen.

My first thought was that this could have been the boy Pixie kissed on Friday night, who, perhaps trying to continue their liaison beyond a single encounter, had exposed himself to a fair degree of ridicule; without realising that no matter how hard he tried, Pixie had probably set her sights on finding someone beyond the confines of the Sailing Club fraternity.

He'll learn. Someone always gets hurt.

~

Steve took a break from filling the drinks fridge and then came over to speak to me.

"Thanks, mate, for grabbing those balloons. You've saved Jill and my butt. We've had big issues with the fridge while you were away. Every time we open the door, it takes forever to return to the set temperature."

With sweat still pouring off me from my recent adventure with the girls, I added. "It's not getting any cooler outside either, mate. But we did have a bit of fun at Lombard's. Anything else I can do?"

Steve then said while pointing at my soaked tee-shirt. "You need a break before you do anything else, mate, and so do I ... a softie?"

I nodded in the affirmative. I did need a drink. Steve returned to the fridge, spoke to Jill, who declined an offer for a rest, and then grabbed two cans of soft drink, before walking back to where I stood, out of everyone's way, and handed me a can.

"They're not real cold, but they're wet," Steve said apologetically. "Come out onto the balcony before the sun hits it."

Steve and I walked out onto the balcony, which still had a hint of the morning's coolness in its shadows and then we stared out onto a bay as flat and as still as glass.

"Nice place to spend summer," I said, before opening my arms and drawing in a large breath of fresh bay air.

"Not bad," Steve replied, as he let his arms flop down onto the balcony rail, his shoulders drooped, and I wondered if he would make it through till midnight.

"You know." Steve said, "I could drop everything right now and dive into that beautiful water. So tempting."

He shook his head and then continued.

"Fee used to love it out here. She'd sit for ages looking out onto the bay. That was before she got busy and had to do stupid things like run off to New South to please some movie pricks … and what's worse this time — at New Year."

Steve pushed off the rail.

"Bloody rubbish."

"Tell me about it," I said and then took a long swig of satisfying, yet lukewarm, orange soft drink.

Steve, who I had never seen so down in the mouth in the short time I had known him, said in a philosophical way.

"You know, you've got to be careful with success. I've

known a few successful people over the years. It has its up-sides and its down-sides. Fee's movie, *The Desert Crossing,* took her away for months. Massive compensation at the Box Office, of course, but the kids were young, and Andy took it as a sign to do whatever he pleased. Sorry, Michael, I shouldn't be talking out of school."

"Everybody's got baggage, Steve," I said in the stoic way a man might close off a dialogue that could reveal any true feelings. After a few moments, I reconsidered.

"What's Andy like?" I asked straight up. "Really like."

"Geez, you've caught me on the hop there," Steve said, and then rubbed his chin, more uncomfortable with that question than with what to do with his dodgy fridge. He looked at me and then turned to face the bay.

"Look. Andy's a great guy. He would do anything for anyone. But, at the end of the day, he liked the final scene ending with him as the hero."

Steve's gaze then returned to me.

"He didn't like Fee's success. He couldn't handle it. His ego was wounded. I suspect that after they split, he made a clean break from the guys around here so the cut would heal quicker."

Steve wiped his mouth. I took this as a sign that he'd told me more than he wanted to.

"I can see some reason in that," I said, wondering if I had made a huge mistake in picking through the dirty laundry of people's lives. "But, it must have been tough times for Fee's kids."

"Yeah, Pixie used to spend a lot of time moping around here then," Steve stated, his mood perking up a tad. "It's a wonder she's not sick of the place."

"I wouldn't know," I said, while also remembering that Pixie had promised me a stick in the eye if I ever repeated her inner thoughts on the club.

"I worry about Pix, sometimes, and Zac, too," Steve said as he re-attached a small patch of bunting to the balcony rail. "I think this thing about Pix having a bad reaction to alcohol has a lot to do with all of us around here focusing too much on it."

"Mind you," Steve added, perhaps realising the inconsistency of his words. "Pix shouldn't be drinking, anyway. She's not eighteen."

"It might be a blessing for her down the track," I added, comfortable without other witnesses to take the high ground on sensible drinking.

"True," Steve said, pushing himself upright and then bending his back.

"Now, not wanting to be a hypocrite, but could you stick around for another hour or so and help us fill a spare fridge with grog? And if you can also pray that none of the fridges shit themselves before the end of tonight's show. That would be great."

The surface of the bay then began to ripple as the hot

Northerly finally arrived. I crushed the soft drink can in my hand as Steve gave me a quick nod to indicate that we'd better get a move on.

~

PART TWO
HAPPY NEW YEAR

1

New Year's Day, 1997. Shortly after midnight

Whoever you are down the road screaming. The New Year is in. Skyrockets have been fired, Auld Lang Syne sung. I don't care if you're having a good time — Piss off!

I rolled over, annoyed after being woken not long after finding deep sleep for the first time in months. I sat up and reached for the glass of water on my bedside table.

The noise faded seconds later as I suspected the culprits had moved on up the road to disturb someone else. *Good!* I had another sip of lukewarm water, found the cool side of my pillow and then laid my head back down.

Sleep take me.

The doorbell rang, then it rang again.

Who the hell is ringing the bloody doorbell at this hour? I should have taken Pixie's advice and cleared off for a few days.

Zac came home early from the New Year's Eve party. He could get it. Then again, it would take nothing short of the house burning down, or a voracious girl waiting in the backyard, for Zac to get up and do anything. It was likely to be Pixie and her mate, Lou, playing silly buggers again.

I peeled the moist cocoon of black silk off me, and then stretched my neck from left to right as I sat on the edge of the bed. I wasn't going to rush. This was probably a prank. I threw on a tee-shirt and an old pair of shorts, swore to myself, and then ventured towards the stairs.

By the time I reached the top of the stairs, there was no more ringing, only banging and yelling at the door. One of the muffled voices could have been Lou's.

Okay, okay, I'm coming!

The doorbell rang again and I could hear Lou's voice clearly now.

"Mr Freeman, can you please open the door?"

You'd better have a good reason for all this racket, Lou.

I descended the staircase cautiously at first and then increased my pace as I saw through the glass panelling of the door, and under the glow of the porch light, three or four figures facing the door; someone was being carried.

Lou then peered through the glass panel with an anguished look on her face, her complexion pale. I switched on the foyer light and then fiddled behind a vase until I found the front door key. After quickly unlocking and then opening the door, I studied the blank looks on the faces of the three adolescents who stood before me; especially the one on the face of a tall teenage boy who shuddered as he cradled in his arms a limp female form in a royal blue dress; her face obscured by blonde hair.

"What's going on? Is that Pixie?" I directed at Lou, only because she stood ahead of the others, then allowed her time to respond.

Lou struggled to find words. I looked again to her right at the tall teen, and then to his left to Tracey; they both looked down, evading my eyes, without giving a response.

Why isn't anyone speaking?

I spoke again to Lou, this time with firmness. "This had better not be a joke, Lou. Not the right time for it — I'm serious."

Lou finally managed to reply through her shallow breath. "It's not a joke, Mr Freeman. It's Pixie. She collapsed on the way home."

Why would she? What is this?

I stepped past Lou and then slowly drew back the blonde hair of the unresponsive girl in the arms of the young man. I didn't immediately recognise this face with eyes firmly shut, devoid of expression; cheeks pale that had never lacked colour before; lips blue, which only hours earlier had sent me an unexpected smile across the hall as she danced with friends.

Anger gripped me.

"Can you give her to me?" I demanded to the young man, who I knew was the same teenager who had approached Pixie late yesterday morning. I reached to take her from him but he held her closer to his chest while taking a hurried step backwards.

Okay, this has just happened. They're all in shock.

I didn't persist but took a step backward myself, to assure him, to calm him. I also needed to calm and reassure myself that taking care of young people was my strength — it's what I do. I took a deep breath, held it in fast and wished to hell that Fiona was here; not to see her unconscious daughter, but to help me make the right decisions in the coming minutes. My lungs could only hang on for so long.

"Does *anybody* know why Pixie collapsed?"

The tall teenager looked down, not willing to meet my eyes. I turned immediately to Lou. Things weren't moving as fast as they should, seconds were playing out like minutes. I had to have an explanation — Now!

"We found Pixie sitting on the sand, further down the beach," Lou said more coherently as she managed to regain some composure. "She was complaining about the heat, then started talking rubbish on the way home and collapsed just down the road." She then threw an arm backwards and pointed in the general direction of the Sailing Club. The exact location perhaps not important.

"Did anyone see her drink alcohol?" I asked, looking for any clue as to what would put Pixie in this state.

"She doesn't drink!" The tall teen snapped. "You don't know her..."

Settle down smart-arse.

"We don't think so, Mr Freeman. Her face would have swollen up by now." Lou replied clearly, rapidly overcoming her anxiety.

I looked to Tracey, who, with her arms crossed and face flushed, had remained silent in the background, appearing to lack the confidence she exhibited on Christmas Eve. She then spoke loudly and deliberately.

"I saw Pix talking to some guys in the carpark, not long before midnight ... They were sharing a bottle of Coke."

Lou then spun around to face her, with a look that said *that's a bloody lie. Pixie would never do that.*

"Did you see these guys?" I asked Lou and then looked directly at the teenager boy.

"I didn't go out to the carpark, Mr Freeman, till we left," Lou replied without hesitation. I had to believe her. The young man shook his head.

Come on, Michael. You have to take Pixie off this young bloke.

"Okay, let's get Pixie inside, mate," I said in the calmest and most composed manner I could muster under circumstances I was struggling to comprehend. Although, I could perhaps understand this boy's feelings;

he wanted to protect someone he likes or thinks he loves. I had to tread carefully.

The boy hesitated. I stepped back and held the door open for him. He stepped forward.

Once inside I again asked if I could take Pixie from him. He agreed by taking another step forward. I passed one arm under her back, the other under the hem of her dress and immediately felt dampness on it. *If Pixie has wet herself, it doesn't matter, it happens.* I supported her head and took the full weight in my arms as the young man stared unemotionally at the side of my face.

Once I held her confidently in my arms, I asked Lou if she could go into the bathroom and grab some towels and place them on Pixie's bed. Before I could take a step to move Pixie to her room, my attention was drawn back to the dampness, its consistency thicker than I had first thought. *Pixie hasn't wet herself.* I discretely rolled her centimetres away from me and looked down to see smears of blood under the hemline of her dress, her legs scratched in random patterns.

God, no...

Bile rose in my throat and strength drained from my arms. I kept telling myself to stay strong and to not let this first impression dominate my thinking. I also couldn't allow the situation, as it was, to go on any longer. Something serious had happened to Pixie. I needed to act quickly.

1

"Tracey, can you grab your mum, please?" I asked as an order.

Tracey gave me an odd look as if questioning the need for her mother to be involved.

"Quick, get her and your dad, too. I want him to take this young man home." Tracey hesitated for a split second, then ran towards her house.

I turned to the tall young man.

"Thanks for looking after Pixie, mate. I appreciate it and I'm sure Pixie will, later, but I want you to head home with Tracey's dad when he gets here."

"My name's Kane, so you know, and I only live in Plummer Road," He said wiping his hands together in an agitated state, and then added. "I can walk home by myself."

"I'm sure you can, but I'd prefer you to wait here and go home with Jerry — Can you do that?"

Kane unwillingly nodded his head, although, with his shoulders slumping and his eyes beginning to glaze over, his limited resistance was understandable. He touched Pixie gently on the shoulder and then said. "I hope you're going to be alright."

"We all do, Kane," I added before carrying Pixie away from him and down the corridor to her room.

~

2

Lou had laid several towels on Pixie's bed and waited attentively for us to enter the bedroom, appearing calm and willing to help her friend. I was grateful for the lack of hysterics. That may not last.

"I'll get a cold face-washer," Lou said in the bright way a good student would. "It might wake her up." Then again left for the bathroom. Lou's support was great, but it was Roz I needed the most; someone who Pixie knew well, and could trust. A mature woman who she could have confidence in and hopefully communicate with about what had left her this way.

I wasn't willing to accept the worst scenario, and hoped at best that this was only Pixie's complex metabolism playing out — but for her, drinking with boys in a carpark close to midnight on New Year's Eve, *was* the nearest thing to insanity she could have ever done.

I carefully laid Pixie on her side in case she vomited, checked her pulse, which was strong, covered a small stain that had appeared at the back of her dress the best I could, and then stood back stunned as I looked upon a face without emotion or movement.

Taking me by surprise was Zac poking his head in through the ajar bedroom door. I had completely forgotten he was in the house.

"What's up, Michael?" Zac asked while yawning and then looked over at Pixie. "Bloody hell, what's happened to Pix?"

"We don't know, mate," I said quietly as Lou returned from the bathroom, face-washer in hand. Lou then added. "Tracey said she saw her drinking Coke with some guys in the carpark. I can't believe she'd do that. Did you see Pix outside the clubrooms?"

"No, the last time I saw her she was dancing with you and Isla … It got too hot and stuffy in the hall, so I went home." Zac said with growing concern for his sister. "There were all sorts of people roaming around the carpark, most of them had drinks in their hand."

Zac shook his head. "…don't know."

Lou knelt down in front of Pixie and began to wipe her face. With her eyes still firmly closed, Pixie lifted her head a centimetre off the towel-covered pillow in response to the cold, or perhaps from being touched, and then laid it quickly down again."

"Come on, Pix. Can you please wake up?" Lou quietly pleaded and then turned to me. "Mr Freeman, we've got to get her to a hospital. And why is Tracey involved? Pixie hates her."

Zac looked away perhaps embarrassed for Tracey as Lou's Pollyanna act came to an abrupt end.

"Tracey knows more about what happened than anyone," I said to Lou, not wanting personal grudges to make us miss a piece of information that may be crucial later.

"Lou, does your mum and dad, or anyone from the club know Pixie's not well?"

"No, we headed straight back here. She seemed alright when we left. We thought it was only the heat — I couldn't believe it when she collapsed."

My thoughts then unwittingly drifted back to the show at the Sailing Club; faces unknown and familiar came in and out of view as I tried desperately to remember anyone or anything that should have raised my concern.

"Mr Freeman, are you okay?" I heard as I felt a hand touching my arm. I shook my head and looked down to see Lou's face.

"Yeah ... Yeah, fine thanks." I replied, annoyed with myself for having lost concentration. "Sorry Lou, could you contact your folks as soon as Mrs Wright gets here and tell them Pixie's unwell. Now, I'm asking you straight. If you want to come with us to the hospital, you have to understand it could be a very long night, and we may not be back here until well into the morning."

Lou took Pixie's hand. I had my answer.

"I can't believe Pixie would take a drink from someone she doesn't know," Zac said, his body beginning to shake as the reality of his sister's condition hit home. "She's so careful with what she drinks."

"Maybe, it wasn't the drink, Zac," I replied to try to ease his mind. "This could just be a reaction to the heat we've been having."

I heard a man's voice and activity at the front door and had to assume it was Tracey returning with her mum and dad. Two sets of footsteps in the hallway signalled Roz and Tracey's return and gave me relief that Kane had finally gone. Roz stepped cautiously in through the bedroom door. Tracey stayed back in the hall.

"Michael, what's going on?" Roz asked, then stared wide-eyed over at the bed with her mouth open, demonstrating the same shock I had felt on first seeing Pixie unconscious. With one hand over her mouth, Roz went over and felt Pixie's brow and then rubbed her arm. I could only give her a few moments to try to gently wake Pixie before I had to move things along.

"Roz, sorry for dragging you out at this hour, but we're going to need your help."

"Okay Michael, tell me what's happened." Roz said as a measured response.

"We're not sure of a lot of things, but we know Pixie

collapsed on the way back from the Sailing Club and Tracey saw her drinking with some guys in the carpark."

"Drinking alcohol?" Roz looked at her daughter and then asked her directly. "Trace, what was Pixie doing with these boys? I need the truth."

Tracey seemed to withdraw into herself, before responding somewhat timidly to her mother.

"She was talking to two guys in the carpark, not long before midnight. They were passing a bottle of Coke or something around."

"Coke, my arse," Roz said angrily while staring at her daughter in a way that suggested she may have been more than a witness.

"Do you know these guys?"

"No, Mum. I definitely do not. They could have been surfies or something. They both had bleached hair and were standing in front of a white panel van with surf-boards on top. I'm sure it was theirs."

"I don't think Pixie would deliberately drink alcohol," I said to try to distract Roz's attention away from her daughter. "The reaction is too bad. It could have been caused by something else."

In reality, I was over speculating if Pixie had drunk alcohol or not, so I jumped in before Roz could add any more.

"Sorry, Roz — Lou, can you call your parents, please. Can you do it now?"

"Okay," Lou replied without question and then headed out of the bedroom door, pushing past Tracey as she headed down the hall towards the family room. Seconds later, Pixie began to throw her arms about and then let out a low groan. Roz went immediately over to the bed and began to cradle her.

"Why did you wait for me, Michael?" Roz asked abruptly.

"Why didn't you take Pixie straight to hospital?"

As Pixie became more agitated and Roz struggled to maintain her hold, the stain at the bottom of her dress and the scratches under the hem, now weeping small lines of blood, became evident. On seeing these, Roz lifted her head and closed her eyes. Zac and Tracey stared in shock. I could only guess at the thoughts that rushed through their minds.

Lou returned to the bedroom carrying another towel and placed it beside the bed before noticing that Roz was now holding Pixie and the mood in the room had deteriorated.

"Did Pix wake up, Mrs Wright?" Lou asked and then looked from one person to the next for an answer.

"She became a little restless," Roz replied quietly, trying to avoid alarm.

"Lou, Pix has some cuts on her... "

Lou turned sharply to look towards Pixie's face and then down at her legs, which now had clear evidence of blood on them. Stunned, she knelt down and began to wipe Pixie's legs with the spare towel.

"Do you think someone's hurt her, Mrs Wright?" Lou asked in a whisper and then caught her breath as she realised the significance of what she had just said.

Roz studied Pixie's tranquil face and then spoke to her with words that mirrored what everyone was thinking.

"Pix, we will do *everything* in our power to make sure you're safe — That's a promise,"

Just as I'd hoped, Roz's calm, self-assurance had begun to turn this terrible situation around.

"Michael, we need to get Pixie to Sandringham Emergency, *now*," Roz said, taking as much control as required. "Ambulances will be flat-out tonight, so we're better off driving straight to Sandringham ourselves."

"It should be less than ten minutes this time of night," I added.

"Pixie mumbled something about her dad before she collapsed," Lou cut in, distracting us from our goal. "He's only in Cheltenham. He should know, he is her dad."

"Okay, Lou. We've got it," Roz replied shortly. "I'll call Andy when I can. Michael, we'll take your car, only because it's bigger. And, you'd better call Fee. Which mightn't be that easy, seeing she's in the bloody Blue Mountains. In my opinion, we should get Pix to the hospital first."

"Okay, but I *have* to phone Fiona as soon as we get

there. She has to know what's going on." I stated, accepting that trying to phone her now could cost us precious time I had already used up.

Roz turned to face her daughter who had remained inconspicuous outside the bedroom door and then said sharply.

"Right — Trace, you can head home now. There's no need for you to be here. Tell your dad I'll see him when I see him."

Tracey seemed hurt by her mother's somewhat cold dismissal, after appearing to have done nothing more than help someone in trouble.

With eyes lowered, Tracey turned and walked down the hall, leaving shortly afterwards by the front door.

"Lou, can you grab a pair of Pixie's pyjamas, some nickers and things." Roz continued. "We will also need to bring in everything she's been wearing ... Just because."

Roz prepared to lay Pixie down again, when Pixie threw an arm backwards without warning, striking Roz with a stunning blow across the face, and then screamed; with words indistinct at first, that soon became clear.

"Michael! — Michael!"

All eyes turned in the direction of the sound and then to me.

"Pix, everything's okay. We're going to take you to hospital." Roz said, quickly shaking off the effects of the blow, but unable to hold Pixie steady or stop her arms from flailing about. I went over to try to wrap Pixie's arms tightly with mine.

"Let's try to lay her down, Michael," Roz said, completely losing her hold on Pixie.

Roz and I struggled to calm Pixie, who then suddenly pushed backward with unexpected force, pinning Roz between bed and wall; as Pixie kicked her legs out violently, her eyes rolled back in her head.

"Let me go, Michael." She screamed, "Stop touching me!"

Pixie scratched my arm before I was able to lay my full weight upon her and allow Roz to slide off the end of the bed. I held Pixie still, resisting any movement until I was sure there was none. Calm gradually returned to Pixie, her breathing steady, before I was able to slowly raise my body off her small frame; a frame that only a minute earlier had been possessed by a powerful demon.

I sensed as soon as I stood that Roz and Lou were regarding me in a different fashion, their eyes avoiding mine. They couldn't possibly believe I was the one responsible for this, just because Pixie had screamed out my name. *Could they?* Whatever their thoughts were, and no matter how unfair I imagined them to be, tonight *had* to be all about Pixie.

"Okay, Lou and I will take it from here," Roz said, her voice directed only at Zac. "Michael, if you and Zac could grab your car out of the garage and clear a space in the back seat that would be great."

Roz then turned her back and returned to Pixie. I patted Zac on the shoulder to urge him to move his growing body out of the bedroom and towards the garage.

~

3

Chaos was expected and that was what confronted us on arrival at Sandringham Hospital. Youths in large groups, many of them inebriated, some hysterical, wandered or staggered their way across the driveway and carpark in the general direction of the hospital entrances.

Like moths to a flame, dozens of people massed below the emergency entrance sign, blocking in the process two ambulance officers trying to push their gurney and its important cargo through the automated doors.

Directly in front of us on the curved driveway, an altercation between a security guard and two men pointing and swearing at him threatened to spill over onto the bonnet of my station wagon. I felt inclined to stop and help this unfortunate guard, but the precarious state of Fiona's daughter took precedence over anyone else's problems. Getting her through to the triage process was the only thing I had to focus on.

In the back seat, Roz sat and cradled Pixie under a

seatbelt. Lou sat close by holding Pixie's hand. On the bench seat beside me, Zac scanned the area for any available parking spaces; all in the vehicle now acutely aware that assistance for our patient may be at the end of a very long queue.

"It'll probably be quicker if I let you out here at the main entrance, Roz. We need to inform the emergency staff as soon as possible that we have an unconscious teen. I'll have to try and find a park out on the street and carry Pix in." I suggested while trying to hide the desperation I was now feeling.

"Going through the mass of people outside the emergency entrance is not an option."

"I can drive," Lou said. "Zac and I will find a carpark if you want to take Pix in now." For a split second, I thought about taking Lou up on her offer and then thought about the consequences for a learner and inexperienced driver, and the person who left them to negotiate this crowd.

"Thanks for offering, Lou, but if you hit someone…" Roz replied before I could, as I contemplated dumping the car where it was; in the middle of the driveway. *How many people would that hurt?*

As if our prayers had suddenly been answered, a car space opened up before us at the end of the curved driveway, a hundred metres from the main entrance. I turned in to it abruptly and didn't dare go forward to straighten. I exited from behind the wheel to the rear passenger side door with only the barest recognition of what I had done.

"I'll take her," I said directly to Roz, as soon as she opened the door and then added.

"Roz, can you please work some magic in the Emergency Department?"

Roz's only reply was 'They have to give children priority', as she left with a look of steely determination. Lou helped pass Pixie out to me, touching the side of her face as I took her safely in my arms. Shortly afterwards, Lou, Zac and I then walked at a steady pace towards the main entrance.

Lou hid her sobbing well, as Zac decided to walk ahead, saying he would try to find a space for us to wait in Emergency; everyone wanting to help in the best way they could. But, it was Roz's ability to make herself heard that Pixie depended upon.

~

With Lou beside me, I carried Pixie towards the din and commotion of an agitated crowd at the entrance to the Emergency Department.

I had only been in this department once before, on the unfortunate occasion, four years ago, of my best mate, Doug, ducking into a low rising bouncer in his Thirds grade cricket match in Hampton. We waited for an hour on a Saturday afternoon to be attended to back then, behind only five or six minor injuries; there were ten times that number tonight, and many with a lot worse trauma.

Zac had found us a space on a bench which followed the curved wall of the corridor at the start of the packed waiting area, twenty metres from the Emergency Reception sign. Zac sat on my left side, Lou on the opposite, her moist eyes continuing to look at Pixie's face and she would not let go of her hand. Zac stared blankly at the heightened anger and over-exaggerated emotions on the faces of those who waited ahead of us; over-indulgence at their own hands causing the majority of their complaints.

All we could do was wait with an unconscious girl who had most likely been given something against her will.

~

At regular intervals, Pixie dug the nails of her free hand into my left arm, gentler than an hour before and without the accompanying screams. As I watched her hand tense and then release, my thoughts returned to how Fiona had dug her nails into my back on Christmas Eve, while in annoyance at not being here for New Year.

Did you know something, Fee?

Every minute now felt like an eternity as we waited for Roz to return with news of when Pixie could be seen by a triage nurse. I began to question myself again on why Pixie had screamed out my name and scratched my arm in the way she did. Roz drew me out of my self-centred thoughts by appearing directly in front of me.

"It's a bloody nightmare down there," Roz said with a heightened sense of awareness. "The lady at the reception window has a half a dozen people talking over her. You know, she's taking it all in and not even batting an eyelid. She did look up when I said we had a girl who we can't wake up. She immediately whispered something to the triage nurse next to her and got back to me immediately. They'll be taking Pix in to be assessed soon."

"Soon!" I replied shortly, frustration beginning to win over the endless supply of patience a teacher is meant to have. "How long's that?

"I don't know, Michael," Roz said shortly in reply. "I'm going to give Andy a call now. You can call Fee after that … if you like."

"Why wouldn't I like to, Roz?" I snapped back.

Why on earth would she say that?

"Sorry, Michael, I didn't mean anything by that. I'm tired. Of course, you want to call, Fee." Roz turned her face away from us. I had said the wrong thing. Roz had been nothing short of amazing tonight.

"Sorry, Roz…" I said as quickly as I could.

"I'll call Andy, now. Okay?" Roz said with a deflated sound in her voice, before heading slowly away towards a payphone situated near the emergency entrance. Lou touched my shoulder.

"You hurt her, Mr Freeman."

"I know, Lou. I'll try to make up for it."

"But, you did the right thing to ask Mrs Wright for help. She's always calm and such a smart person." Lou said as she sat up close to me while looking at Zac, who had succumbed to sleep on my shoulder. Lou then looked directly at me.

"One thing you should know, Mr Freeman. Mrs Wright got stuck in the middle of all the crap when Pixie's folks broke up. The whole family relied upon her — It was bullshit, really."

A male orderly with slumped shoulders and a permanently tired look on his face arrived out of the crowd with a gurney.

"Okay folks, your girl's been bumped." The orderly said with an upbeat voice which in no way resembled his looks. "They're going to assess her on the way to Resus."

"Thanks, mate," I said through a sigh of relief.

I stood and with the aid of a just woken, Zac, carefully placed a motionless Pixie on the gurney. Zac helped pull up the guardrail as the orderly covered her with a light blanket. I sat back down exhausted, unable to stop my eyes closing as I felt myself drift into sleep against my will.

My body was moving from side to side as the over-whelming feeling of not belonging here, and not being worthy of taking care of someone else's family member, filled my mind.

I'm not family.

I woke to see Zac over me, shaking my shoulders. I looked past him to see Lou standing beside the gurney, rubbing Pixie's arm; the orderly putting light straps over her slim body.

"Pixie has to go in, Mr Freeman," Lou said quietly to me.

"Okay. I'm coming." I said, struggling to maintain balance as I went to stand.

"We gotta go…" The orderly replied sharply, perhaps having put up with enough of everything this evening.

"I want to go in with you," Zac said with a clarity that could not be mistaken for anything but wanting to be there for his sister.

"I'll be going in with you, Zac," Roz said returning from around the curved corridor, just as the orderly was preparing to push the gurney further into the emergency area.

"Andy's on his way, Michael," Roz continued with indifference, giving me the feeling that I had lost a great deal of respect by my careless words.

"He's half-tanked, so his girlfriend's driving him in." Roz then addressed Lou directly.

"Can you wait here with Mr Freeman, for Pixie's dad and his partner to arrive?" Lou was about to reply, to probably plead a case to accompany them, but Roz put up her pointer first.

"Lou, I'm asking you. I want you to tell Mr Farnes that Pixie is unconscious after she collapsed on the way home. That's all. Nothing about surfies or drinking in the carpark, or anything else. We can't say anything until we know more — Okay?"

Lou nodded her acceptance as she reluctantly let go of Pixie's hand.

"Mr Freeman is going to phone Mrs Farnes now, so hold our spot here."

The orderly then gave the gurney a shove from behind and began to forge a passage for Zac and Roz to follow through the gradually depleting casualties of New Year's Eve.

~

4

The lack of a ringtone returning from Fiona's satellite phone to the hospital's somewhat antiquated payphone had me concerned. As did Fiona's isolated location in a valley near Turon Gates on the far side of the Blue Mountains. It made me realise how much of a bad call it was, to not insist on phoning her before we left home.

Another mistake.

I placed the receiver down, grabbed my fifty-cent coin, picked up the receiver again and then put the coin back in the slot. I hit *redial* and after a long silence, a ringtone echoed back to me.

~

In the inky-black interior of a bush cabin, built to replicate a mid-nineteenth century drover's hut, all occupants of twelve camp beds, set out in two rows, slept soundly. A noise similar to but sharper than the ringtone of a landline then resonated throughout the hut.

Fiona poked her head out into the cold night air from under the cover of a thick quilted doona in the closest bed to the draughty entrance. She searched throughout the murky darkness for the source of this annoyance, only able to make out through squinted eyes the silhouettes of disturbed sleepers. Fiona then realised the sound emanated from directly below her, in a backpack that held her satellite phone. She turned on a small campers light.

"Sorry guys," Fiona said quietly to her co-habitants in the cabin, who quickly returned their heads under the warmth of their doonas.

Who the fuck...? She thought before stretching an arm out from the cosy warmth, unzipping the main compartment of the backpack and then pulled out an awkwardly shaped and heavy handset.

"Hello?" Fiona asked with the uncertainty of someone not expecting a call in the middle of the night, so far from home.

"Fee?" Michael asked.

"Yes..." Fiona replied cautiously.

"It's me, Michael ... How are you?"

"Good, thanks, Michael." Fiona replied, shaking her head to try to gain more clarity, "You do know what time it is don't you."

Then with increased awareness that this was perhaps only her intoxicated partner missing her.

"Happy New Year by the way. I hope it wasn't too boring for you at the Sailing Club. We had a bit of fun here, a couple of reds disappeared. But, I haven't been able to stop thinking about you and the kids."

"I've really missed you, too, and Happy New Year," Michael returned. Fiona immediately noticed the lack of enthusiasm in his voice and waited until Michael spoke again.

"Fee, the night hasn't been so uneventful. Now, don't think the worst, but I'm at Sandringham Hospital. We've taken Pixie there."

Fiona sat abruptly up in bed.

"What!" Fiona shouted into the handset. "What are you talking about, Michael? What's Pixie doing in hospital? — She's alright, isn't she?"

Several of the inhabitants in the dormitory also sat up in their beds and looked towards Fiona with concern.

"She's in with the doctors at the moment, Fee." Michael replied calmly, "She's okay. We think she may have drunk something that has given her a bad reaction."

"Pixie's very careful with what she drinks. Are you sure this happened at the Sailing Club? You were there, weren't you?"

"I was, but I went home about eleven. Apparently, she

was talking to some boys outside later in the night. Roz, Zac and Lou came with me to take Pix to the hospital."

"Is Roz there? Can I speak to her?"

"Zac and Roz went into Resus with Pixie. I can check, but I don't…"

"Resus!" Fiona shouted over me. "Is Pix unconscious, Michael? What the hell is going on there? I want you to tell me *everything* that's happened."

I waited for the echo of her last few words to stop reverberating down the line.

"Pix hasn't woken up properly since she collapsed on the way home from the Sailing Club. Lou, Tracey, and a young bloke named Kane brought her home. Fee, I'm not sure you'll want to hear this, but Pix has some scratches on her."

Michael put another fifty-cent coin in the payphone and waited for a response.

"Did she cut herself when she fell?" Fee asked in a hopeful way.

"No, Fee." Michael said slowly, "She's received some cuts."

"I don't like what you're telling me, Michael?" Fiona's voice now reflecting her increased anxiety. "I'm starting to freak out here."

"It's best to stay calm, Fee."

"Best to stay calm — Are you fucking serious!" Fiona shouted as she exited the bed and began to pull clothes out of a travel bag. "Didn't you say you'd stay at the club until midnight? … I knew something would go wrong."

The deep voice of an American man called out from the far end of her row.

"Are you okay, Fiona?"

'Everything will be fine when I get home, Roy.' she called back and then returned to speak into the handset. Michael spoke first.

"Fee, why are you saying something would go wrong? This is just as big a shock for us here."

"I didn't say it's your fault, Michael," Fiona said, her thoughts now lost in worry for her daughter,

"I'm coming home. Does Andy know? Oh, God, I hope no-one's given her any alcohol. Make sure Pixie's alright, Michael. Tell Pix and Zac I love them and I'll be..."

The phone then went silent. Michael stood staring at the gold payphone, unwilling to hit *Follow On* to call Fiona back.

~

5

I returned dejected from around the curved corridor, to see Roz sitting between Lou and Zac in a somewhat subdued emergency area.

"How's Fiona, Michael?" Roz asked before I could ask about Pixie's condition. "This will be doing her head in,"

I replied that it was and then added, "I don't know if I got it across the way I wanted to about what's going on here ... Shit, we have little idea ourselves." I then turned to face Zac.

"Zac, your mum wanted me to tell you that she loves you and will be home as soon as she possibly can ... okay." I said while placing an arm over his shoulder and sitting down beside him.

"Thanks ... I'm glad she'll be back soon." Zac said appreciatively, impressing me with the resilience he had already shown in supporting his sister.

"What did they say in Resus?" I asked Roz.

"Not much," she replied. "They didn't want to

elaborate on anything beyond saying they'd be taking blood samples and running some more tests. They told us to leave while they gave Pix a full examination. One of the nurses said as we left that they treat it as major if a patient remains unconscious for any length of time."

My attention was then drawn to the deep, booming voice of a man who was pushing his way through groups of people at the emergency entrance. The tall and unkempt man marched ahead of a slim busty woman of Greek appearance. I had seen this man before, only once, and at a distance, but I knew it was Andy. He noticed Zac, and then Roz, and made large strides towards them.

"Zac, you right, mate?" Andy asked loudly with a slur in his voice, making heads turn nearby. He hugged Zac and then over his shoulder spoke to Lou.

"How are you, young lady? Sorry, I've forgotten your name."

"I'm Lou, remember from…?"

Before Lou could say any more, Andy had turned to Roz.

"Roz, what the heck's goin' on with Pix? ... By the way, this is Joan."

Andy kissed Joan on the forehead and then saw me sitting further down the bench, hoping to remain anonymous. He stretched out his long right arm and aimed his pointer.

"You!" Andy shouted with a boorish sneer. This time

all nearby stopped and stared. "Don't go anywhere. I wanna talk to you."

Zac, uneasy about his father's outburst, lowered his dad's arm. I hesitated before I walked directly towards, and then up close to Andy's face.

"I'm not going anywhere, Andy, until I know Pixie's safe," I said calmly and then sensed that this man was nothing more than a garden variety bully, and wouldn't like to be stood up to.

I took a chance and leant my head further forward, wanting to say 'You're nothing but a big-mouthed prick', then whispered something he deserved more,

"So, you're the bloke who walked out on his family."

Andy pulled sharply away from me, his face immediately taking on the crimson of a man who only knew aggression. I knew he wanted to hit me — but he couldn't — because everyone in the emergency area was watching him now; including his son, his former neighbour, his daughter's best friend — and also, his new partner, Joan.

"Don't worry, we'll talk again, teacher boy," Andy said with little conviction, appearing now somewhat lost and confused. "And you won't like the outcome." He then pushed past me further into the Emergency Department.

"Joan, I'm going to see Pix," Andy called back to his new partner, whose face showed discomfort from the unwanted attention, "Can you wait here, love?"

After Andy had taken a few steps, he stopped and

then surprisingly turned back to face us. He contemplated the crowd that looked at him with astonishment for the unnecessary drama he had created and then spoke directly to Roz without any attempt to impress.

"You might think I'm the bad guy here, Roz, but you don't know this man." Andy again pointed at me.

"He should *never* have been left alone with my kids."

~

6

I told Roz, Lou, and Zac that I needed to have a walk outside to get some fresh air; and I did, but I also needed time to think. I was fairly sure I knew what Andy was getting at with his 'you don't know this man' speech. If I was correct, it was an incident that was the lowest point in my working life, and close to the worst in my private; only the separation from my wife upset me more.

I took the cup of vending machine coffee I had purchased near the main entrance, through that entrance, then found a quiet spot to drink it, next to my station wagon. Andy had been in with Pixie for over an hour, and I began to second-guess every decision I had made tonight, hoping that that none of them had exacerbated Pixie's already dangerous condition.

From my location, I could then see Roz stride out of the main entrance, look around from under the glare and swarming insects of its sign, until noticing me wave to her. She walked briskly over, asked how I was, and then relaxed against the side of the wagon.

"The vending machine coffee's not much chop, is it?" Roz stated with no apparent animosity after Andy's outburst.

"Milky rubbish — Heard anything?"

"Nothing yet." Roz replied, then pushed off the wagon, stepped in front of me and said the expected phrase, "The waiting's the worst part." Then brought up the real reason she searched me out.

"Can you please tell me what Andy was on about inside — before he does? Because you know, he'll try to make you look like shit every opportunity he can."

I studied my feet wishing none of this was real.

"I already feel like crap that I didn't make sure Pixie got home safe after the show, Roz — and her reaction to me in the bedroom. I can't believe that happened."

"It didn't look good," Roz said bluntly.

"I'm sure it didn't. But the crazy thing is, I've got no explanation for why she would scream out my name — Not a single thing."

Roz looked towards the main entrance and then prepared herself for what she was about to say.

"Michael, if someone has assaulted Pixie, the police and God knows who else will get involved. People will start pointing fingers, and you're the new kid on the block."

Great! Now, I'm guilty of attacking my partner's daughter.

"I know, but you know what? People make up their minds on these sort of things regardless of the facts. So why try...?"

Roz moved her head to match the avoidance of my eyes.

"I don't know you that well, Michael, but you're coming across as a weak prick by saying that — Pixie's in Emergency and you're the one who needs a tissue."

Piss off, Roz. I was the one singled out.

I couldn't avoid the subject any longer and I should have known it would come out eventually. It was better to tell someone who might listen.

"What Andy's probably on about, and who knows what he's trying to prove, but I think it's about an incident that occurred a few years back, and it involved a female student. Sorry, two female students. And it's something I haven't told Fiona about, yet. Which I can now see is a big friggin mistake."

I walked over to a nearby bin and threw my paper cup in, before returning to Roz, who seemed to anticipate what I was about to say.

"Okay, over two years ago, a Year-Twelve student used a friend to make it look like we were having an affair *and* that I had touched her inappropriately. She had a crush, and set me up — Quite well, actually."

"Michael..." Roz said quietly, looking at me dumbfounded.

~

7

Linda squinted as she gazed into the mirror of the small compact her mother had given her the first day she showed an interest in makeup.

She touched up her foundation so that her skin was blemish-free, applied red lipstick to her pouted lips, rouge to her high-boned cheeks and then ran her fingers lightly over what she believed to be her curved-in-all-the-right-places figure until she reached the higher than regulation hem of her blue and gold check Frankston High School uniform.

She knew she had her best friend, Mel, covered for looks; even if the latter had decided to put on something better than a baggy tracksuit.

"How do I look, bee-arch?" Linda asked as she turned side-on to Mel, and then produced an array of modelling moves to show she was a class above; an unusual display on a nature strip, on the opposite side of the road to a soul-less suburban rental flat.

"Did you know my mum was a catwalk model?" Linda added only to brag.

Mel shook her head and then dug deep into her cram-packed canvas bag, pulling out a small paper bag pressed into the shape of a flask.

"You're fuckin' stupid." Mel said in exasperation at her friend's over-the-top antics, "Have a swig of this. It might sort out your thick head."

Linda, then snatched the paper bag from Mel, ripped open the wrapping; twisted the metal cap anti-clock-wise until it came away and fell to the ground; then with urgency lifted the bottle to her mouth.

Linda's eyes lit up before she spat out half of her first-ever swig of brandy, coughing repeatedly at the ground until she was able to catch her breath and then threw the bottle back towards Mel.

"Oh, fuck! My throat is on friggin' fire."

Linda winced as she wiped her mouth with her right arm, and then with a screwed up face reached into a small plastic bag containing the disposable camera she had just purchased from a nearby chemist.

"Have a looky at what I got," Linda said, exhibiting an extra glow on her rouged cheeks. "Even a goody-two-shoes like you could use this little baby."

Linda smirked as she threw the Kodak Funsaver to

Mel, who pretended it was a hot potato, catching it just above the ground.

"Oops! Look what you nearly made me do, slag bag." Mel said and then pretended to take a snap of Linda. "I almost dropped your looney plan."

Linda went quiet as the gravity of what lay ahead, hit home. "I want to do this, but I don't." She said quietly with her arms open wide, hoping for a hug from Mel, who she wished would be more supportive.

"You know, Mr Freeman is never going to talk to you again if you go through with this photo shit," Mel said.

"Ha! — You're takin' the photos," Linda replied smugly as if catching her out,

"And he'll have to. The evidence'll be on the reel."

"Don't you get it, he doesn't like you." Mel said, holding Linda tightly by the shoulders and looking directly into her eyes to make sure she paid full attention, "He feels sorry for you because you're such a dumbo. He's only trying to teach you somethin' — Got it?"

"Mel! — Just click, click, click — bitch, bitch, bitch."

The two girls then hugged, a nervous laugh came from Linda before she ran excitedly across the road. She looked back as soon as she reached the front door of the rental flat to make sure Mel was ready to signal.

Linda pressed the cobweb-covered doorbell and moved out of sight behind clinker brickwork. A minute later, Michael opened the interior door but kept the security door locked. He looked around the near vicinity, barely able to see through the dusty grill.

"Hello ... is there anybody out there?" Michael asked in a ghoulish Roger Waters' way and then had to smile at his own poor humour.

Probably knick-knockers. Michael thought and then heard a barely audible giggle.

Okay, smarty, let's see who you are.

Michael opened the security door, but before he had time to peer around the brickwork, he noticed a girl waving in his direction from the nature strip on the opposite side of the street; who he soon recognised as one of his students, Mel Sullivan.

He was about to wave back and call out to her but was distracted by a blur of movement to his right. Mel lifted the camera and clicked at the same time as Linda raced under Michael's arm and into his flat.

Through the viewfinder, it looked as if Michael had let Linda in.

Seconds later, as Michael gently led Linda outside by the arm, Mel sighted for another shot and then clicked; the shot when developed seemed to show a distressed Linda being dragged out of his flat.

"Go home now, Linda, and this never happened," Michael said firmly to a girl, silent, but in no way distraught.

"If you don't, I will call your parents, our principal, and the police, in that order — You're choice."

Linda lowered her head and nodded in agreement. Michael let go of her arm and then said quietly.

"Okay, see ya at school on Monday."

Michael patted Linda on the shoulder and then indicated with a movement of his head in Mel's direction that she should leave as well. During this time, Mel had taken one final photo. It will appear, although blurred, that Michael's hand was over Linda's breast.

In the house behind Mel, an old man in a flannel shirt and overalls was standing in the front garden of his home pruning a rose bush and watching with interest Michael's interaction with Linda. Uncomfortable with what he believed to be a teenage girl being threatened, he left his property and then stood beside Mel to get a better look. When it appeared that Michael had touched Linda inappropriately, the pensioner then rushed across the road to intervene.

"Hey, you big man!" The man in his late seventies called out. "Don't do that to a young girl."

The neighbour stepped onto the rental property and then in between Linda and Michael.

"Everything right with you, young lady? Let me know if it ain't." The old man asked Linda. Before she had a chance to explain the truth, he was in Michael's face.

"Don't worry, he's not much this fella," The pensioner

shouted so that both girls and the whole street could hear, and then commenced to breathe heavily. "Too good to talk to his neighbours. That's what I've noticed."

"Go home now, Linda, and keep up your studies," Michael yelled past the old man.

Linda dashed across the road to join Mel; they hugged briefly, before running off.

"You're not getting out of scaring a girl that easy." Michael's neighbour said, his voice now shallow and weak. "I'm calling the police on you."

"No need to do that, mate. My student has gone home and so should you — Nothing to see here." Michael said, his hands raised and open to show he wanted no aggression.

"Smartarse, just as I thought." The neighbour tried to yell and then took a swing at Michael, who stepped easily out of range. The old man fell forward and would have landed on his outstretched arm if Michael hadn't caught him first.

Michael lowered the old man, who now held a hand over his chest, onto the ground and then proceeded to sit him upright.

"Do you want me to call an ambulance, mate?" Michael asked in a calming manner. "Or, would you like me to take you home?"

His neighbour hesitated for a moment, looked at the ground and then said while nodding his head.

7

"I'll be right if ya can get me home, so I can knock down some medicine."

Michael carefully lifted the old man, and then with an arm around his waist, helped him across the road.

~

8

New Year's Day, 1997. Early morning

"I thought the matter was done and dusted, but Linda was showing everyone at school the photos Mel took. Of course, word got back to the principal. I was called in immediately and interviewed by him, without an ounce of favour *or* sympathy on his behalf. After going over it several times, he eventually accepted that I was telling the truth. He had to notify the police, of course. Mandatory Reporting and all that shit. Which I was fine with."

Roz glared at me.

"Michael, are you stupid? You should have told Fiona about this — Jesus, you're alone with her teenage children."

"I know, Roz. I know. I was planning to tell her when she got back."

Roz looked away as she shook her head. "Oh, well! That's way too bloody late now."

"Roz, for me it was over two years ago." Trying to emphasise that I had to move on before it dragged me down. "Young Melanie blurted out that they'd set me up as soon as her parents were called in to see the Principal."

"It doesn't matter," Roz said, turning back sharply to look at me. "Shit like that sticks. Andy will make sure all the neighbourhood knows about it. Don't hide stuff, Michael."

No sooner had Roz stopped berating me than Lou walked rapidly out through the main entrance door, noticed us and then followed the curved footpath around until she stood beside Roz; tears running down her cheeks while looking guardedly over at me.

"Mr Farnes says they're taking Pix to the Alfred," Lou said quietly as her voice began to falter. "The doctor told him she'd been drugged."

Lou leant her head against Roz's shoulder and was then in turn taken into her arms. I turned away, the wind knocked out of me as if struck heavily to the chest. I lowered my head and then rubbed the back of my neck, feeling sick inside for having let Fiona and her family down.

After fighting to regain some composure, I raised my eyes towards the sky and noticed daylight breaking over the houses along Bluff Road.

"Zac's going with his dad in the ambulance. Mr Farnes says I need to go home. He says I look exhausted." Lou murmured, barely able to lift her head off Roz's chest. She did need to go home, as we all did. Pixie was under the best care possible and there was nothing more we could do.

Lou then said to Roz. "He said Joan would take us home."

Roz lifted Lou away from her chest and looked closely at her.

"Did he say why Joan would take us?" Roz asked, just as mystified as me by what Andy had requested.

"We all came in the same car." Roz continued to Lou, who had lowered her eyes. "There's no need for Joan to go out of her way. Mr Freeman can take us home."

Lou maintained her gaze at the footpath; anywhere but Roz, or me.

"Mr Farnes insisted…" Lou replied quietly. "He says it was in our best interest."

"In the best interest of who?" I interrupted loudly, and out of annoyance at being unfairly insulted; drawing attention to myself from a large group leaving the main entrance.

"Why, because I can't be trusted long enough to drive you home. Because I can't look after the people I'm in charge of?"

Lou had already walked several metres away from me, but I continued to shout so she could hear me.

"I don't know Pixie's father and I don't want to…" I

then began to pace beside my car, and even if it gave the impression that I was no longer in control of my emotions, continued to shout towards the main entrance.

"But he's got me wrong."

As I started to walk towards that entrance, Roz grabbed me by the arm with a grip that surprised me with its strength.

"Shut up, Michael! You're frightening her and you are *not* going anywhere," Roz said firmly, with a look of outrage on her face.

"Andy only does things that suit him and it suits him to turn people against you — and you're helping him — I'll go in."

Roz let go of my arm and then tapped my shoulder with the same hand before she went to join Lou, who stood a short distance from the main entrance.

Ten minutes later, Roz returned alone.

"Let's go, Michael," Roz muttered to herself while walking past me to the passenger side of my wagon. I knew from her body language that she didn't want to engage.

However, I wanted to. "Where's Lou?"

Roz spun around to face me with a look that said she wanted to scream or throw something at me, then thought better of it.

"Do you *really* need to ask?" Roz said as she tried in vain to open the wagon's faulty passenger side door, before quickly giving up.

"Just let Joan drop her home."

~

9

New Year's Day, 1997. Early afternoon

My eyes opened to darkness.

I was lying on my back, the silk sheet below me soaked with perspiration; the doona above suffocating, the tastes of stale beer and horrible coffee mixed in my dry throat; an annoying buzzing sound injuring my ears.

What corner of hell is this?

I threw the doona off my head and was instantly blinded by rays of sunlight streaming in through open windows. With one hand shielding my eyes, I sat myself up.

"Jesus, Fee. What is that bloody sound?"

I felt deflated as I glanced left to see that both the warm body and welcoming smile of Fiona were no longer there. I had been left alone with the high-pitched ringtone from her cordless phone.

I shuffled my body over to Fiona's bedside table and then grabbed the handset from its charger.

"Fee?" I inquired cautiously, not actually sure where she was.

"No, Michael. Sorry," Came a reply from a familiar voice, "It's Roz, I'm at the Alfred."

"Roz…" and then my memories of last night began to flood back like a nightmare.

"Yes, Roz. Remember we took Pixie to Sandringham Emergency last night."

"Roz, yes, of course, I do. Unfortunately, it's all coming back to me." I said, forcing myself to sit upright on the edge of the bed while fighting the urge to drift off into sleep again.

"How's Pixie? Has she woken?"

Roz replied with a degree of excitement. "She has. Still very groggy, though. I was so relieved when Andy came out and told me the good news a couple of hours ago. I tried to phone you then, but you didn't pick up."

"I must have been completely zonked out, Roz," I said, stretching my neck from side to side, wishing I was more lucid.

I jumped off the edge of the bed and began to pace the sun-drenched master bedroom in my boxers. With the cordless handset to my ear, I peered out its large windows at a cloudless sky, unconcerned by my exposure to the neighbourhood.

"That's wonderful, Roz. I was so worried Pixie wouldn't wake at all. Can she remember anything of last night?"

"Nothing much at the moment. Andy said she came around about ten in Intensive Care, completely distressed by what had happened to her. She only remembers a few sketchy things like dancing with Lou at the show."

"I know it's not my place to ask, but was Lou right when she said Pixie had been given a drug?" I asked, not expecting, but hoping to be told the truth.

Roz hesitated at the end of the line for quite a while before she replied. "The staff looking after Pix are very tight-lipped and are keeping contact with her to a bare minimum. But from the small amount I've gathered from Andy and I probably shouldn't be telling anyone this … they did find a drug in her system."

"A date-rape drug?" I asked without reluctance, sensing it had to be the case.

"Yep. It's everywhere at the moment." Roz replied in the exasperated way a person who deals with the unpleasant side of humanity on a day-to-day basis would.

"Where I work in welfare, we're seeing more of these types of cases every month." She then broke off our conversation and spoke to someone with a female voice. Within seconds she returned.

"Fiona's made contact with the Alfred and will be here in the next half an hour. If she calls you before then, please don't mention the *d*-word. Let the doctors tell her."

"Got it, loud and clear. I will be heading in as soon as I can."

Then I remembered a young man who stayed strong for his sister.

"How's Zac?"

"Good. You know what he's like, doesn't stay phased for long. But everyone has their limit." The line then went quiet as I suspected another person had approached Roz. Thirty seconds later she got back to me.

"Andy's going home when Pixie gets moved to a ward, which he said would be soon, so if Zac wants to go home, he'll take him. Okay, better go home myself. Jerry's not keen on hospitals."

"Thanks for keeping me in the loop, Roz. A lot of people would have shut me out. Much appreciated."

"Bye, for now, Michael," Roz replied without a hint of uncertainty in her voice.

I heard Roz place the payphone down and felt immense relief that Pixie was finally conscious and able to communicate to medical staff about what she knew of last night. I placed the handset back onto its charger and sat again on the side of the bed.

I covered my eyes with the palms of my hands and tried to rationalise what on earth would make some people want to drug and assault another person.

What sort of person does that?

However, I wasn't convinced that the young men

9

Pixie was seen drinking with were responsible for drugging her. Sometimes the obvious — is too obvious — maybe it *was* just a bottle of Coke — and why didn't I notice them when I left for home?

Too many things weren't making sense about last night. Why did three people who normally wouldn't be seen dead together, end up bringing Pixie home, and only one them her friend?

I again walked over and stepped into the frame of the large window which looked out over the bay and began to draw closed the heavy curtains when I noticed Tracey standing on the nature strip outside her home staring up at me. I presumed her parents would have contacted her from the Alfred, to let her know the latest.

I gave Tracey the thumbs up to indicate that it was a good thing that Pixie was okay. Without the slightest acknowledgement, Tracey turned her face away and then headed in the direction of the beach.

~

10

Quickly shaved and showered, I was now eager to head into the Alfred Hospital to support Pixie, Fiona and Zac, while at the same time trying to push to the back of my mind the distress of last night; distress which included the negativity of my phone conversation with Fiona.

Why did she think something would go wrong? Where did that come from?

Fiona didn't seem to have any concerns about being away from home at Christmas, and if she did, why not tell me about them, because I would have moved heaven and earth to dispel any fears she had. Nevertheless, I would never mention last night's conversation, unless Fiona did.

~

I slowly backed my station wagon out of the driveway, concentrating on the passenger side mirror to help me steer through our skinny crossover when I heard a rap on the roof. I pulled up sharply. Turning to my right I could see Steve and his tuffs of swept-back hair peering in through the driver's side window; Jill, stood tall in another maxi dress, a metre behind.

"How ya doin', mate?" Steve asked as a muffled sound through the glass; a concern on his face. Jill gave me a small wave from around him.

I'm not sure I need this now.

It would not be possible to know what picture Lou had painted of last night, but it would be difficult to judge someone who had spent the whole night worrying if their partner's daughter was ever going to wake again.

I unbuckled my seatbelt and then stepped out of the car, hoping I didn't have to go over again the awful events of last night.

"I'm alright," I said shaking Steve's hand. Jill stepped around Steve and pressed her cheek against mine. I then realised that they too would have had a long night worrying about their child.

"How's Lou?" I asked, so grateful for the way she cared for Pixie, even though she may not feel so grateful for my late-night outburst. "She was so good with Pixie last night."

"She's still asleep, Michael, completely exhausted. I had to sit with her in bed until she stopped crying and dozed off. We think we should keep her at home with us for a few days," Jill said as she placed a hand on Steve's shoulder,

"She said she can't remember why Andy's girlfriend dropped her off this morning, which I couldn't quite understand — She did leave with you."

Thankfully, Steve cut in before it was necessary to explain.

"I can't help but think how disgusting it is to drug someone," He said bitterly mirroring my earlier thoughts; his fist clenched by his side.

"These guys never thought for one second about the devastating effects drugs can have on people. It's absolute selfishness. I'm so pissed-off, Michael."

"So am I, Steve, but we've got to be careful. We can't go around making accusations. It may not have been the guys Tracey saw Pixie talking to. Pix might know them through sailing and was just having a chat." I said while noticing out of the corner of my eye, Trev standing with his kids, Isla and Beau, in the driveway of their home.

"What was Tracey doing watching her, anyway?" Jill asked, although more interested in whether Trev and his kids would head our way; she then had to add,

"She's not even a friend."

This conversation had begun to drift away from the positive. Who likes who, no longer mattered.

"I heard from the Alfred about an hour ago that Pixie

was awake and talking to staff. She can't remember a lot and I'm sure it will take time before her memory returns." I said wanting to give them something more optimistic to think about. Steve quickly replied.

"We already know it's going to be tough for a while. So, we're going to back off and give Fee and her family as much space as they need."

Steve turned to Jill and then put his arm around her waist. "Aren't we?"

Jill nodded her head and said. "Please pass on our best when you get to the hospital."

"I will," I replied genuinely. "As you can see, Trev and the kids are coming. Can you...?"

Steve and Jill indicated with a short nod of their heads that they knew what was required.

"We'll tell Trev what he needs to know," Steve replied.

"Thanks for that." I responded, appreciative of their understanding.

~

"What's happening neighbours?" Trev's distinctive deep voice called out from the back of my wagon, as his son and daughter felt the need to bang on the tailgate.

"Everyone pull up alright?"

Trev then came up to Jill and greeted her with a kiss on the cheek, shortly afterwards shaking Steve and my hands. I had to assume Trev knew nothing about last night.

"Seems like something's going on here," Trev added with a smile, looking suspiciously at Steve, Jill, and me. I felt I should give Trev something even if it was only an abridged version of the truth.

"We were just talking about how I had to take Pixie into hospital after the show last night, she wasn't feeling well. The doctors want to keep her in there as a precaution, but I'm sure she'll be fine."

"That's no good," Trev said casually, but also aware that things weren't completely as they should be.

Trev then asked. "Is Fee coming back?" Sensing it could be the case.

"I believe she's at the hospital now," I replied, grateful he didn't want to inquire further. "Speaking of which, I should be getting a wriggle on."

"C'mon, Dad," Isla said in her usual whingey way. "I was meant to be at the club half an hour ago to help the Tackers clean up."

Steve then walked over and rubbed Isla on top of the head, saying.

"Jill and I are going to the club right now if you'd like to join us," Isla and Beau then looked over at their dad.

"Alright, alright, I'm coming!" Trev exclaimed as he tacked onto the tail of the departing group. He then turned back and said.

"Get going, Michael. The hospital won't come to you."

~

11

I again turned to look through the passenger side mirror of my wagon, during my second attempt to leave for the Alfred, while contemplating the impact this incident was already having on the neighbourhood, when a white van moved across my vision. I pulled up sharply.

Bloody idiot?

I hopped out of my wagon ready to give the driver a serve, when I realised the car at fault was actually a police divisional van, which had now backed into the vacant parking spot in front of the wind-swept ti-tree on our nature strip; two police officers exited the van: one male, one female.

With doubt about the reason for this visit, I moved towards the back of my wagon to greet them and then thought.

Maybe they've found the two guys.

The female officer, young, tall and athletic, a striking woman, walked casually towards me. After firmly closing the passenger side door; a middle-aged male officer, heavyset and moustached, caught up to her.

Their casual dress of peaked caps, white shirts and blue pants, wasn't what I expected — and I wasn't expecting police officers. They both smiled as they reached me.

The policewoman spoke first. "Mr Freeman?"

"Yes..."

"I'm Detective Inspector, Heather Clarke, and this is my partner, Detective Senior Constable, Brian Wallace." They both leant forward and shook my hand.

These are not the same type of cops I ran into when I was younger.

"Sorry about cutting you off." The policewoman continued with an apology. "Parking's at a premium around here."

"Sure is this time of year," I acknowledged, looking around at the multitude of cars in our street as a brief distraction, while also noticing Tracey standing in her front yard observing us. I then added.

"How can I help?"

"Where from the *SOCIT* unit in Moorabbin." Det. Insp. Clarke answered in a professional and friendly manner. "Can we have a word?"

"Sure ... Although, I was about to go into the Alfred," I said, trying half-heartedly to see if I could put their visit off. "This is about Pixie, isn't it?"

Both officers stared blankly at me while maintaining consistent smiles.

"I'll put the wagon back in the drive."

"Thanks," said Det. Insp. Clarke.

After parking my car, I walked back around to the officers.

"What does *SOCIT* mean?" I asked while gathering that Det. Insp. Clarke would be doing the bulk of the talking.

"It means we're from a sexual assault and child abuse unit." She replied. "It's fairly new. Can we go inside?"

"Sure…" I agreed without a choice, directing them onto the porch and then through the front door. In the hallway, they stopped briefly to look around Pixie's room, before proceeding into the family room to continue their surveillance.

"Mr Freeman, where would be the best place to chat?" Det. Insp. Clarke asked, already moving towards the breakfast bench and the four chairs spaced evenly along its length. I pointed in that direction.

"You can call me, Michael, if that's allowed," I said a touch smartly and then remembered they were my guests,

"Would anyone like a cup of tea or coffee?"

I cleared away my belated breakfast dishes while waiting for a response. The two officers found seats; Det. Insp. Clarke sat on the seat closest to where my dishes had been. Det. Sen. Const. Wallace sat on the seat further away.

"I'm right for coffee, thanks." Det. Insp. Clarke finally

replied. Det. Sen. Const. Wallace shook his head in the negative.

"Michael, you are obviously aware of what occurred last night with Patricia, and if you haven't been contacted by anyone at the Alfred, she is awake and being cared for in Ward 4 AMU. Also, a child protection officer from *SECASA* has been called in as support." Det. Insp. Clarke stated, revealing another acronym I hadn't heard of before.

"That's great news. I actually spoke to Roz, the lady who helped me last night, about an hour ago. She told me Pixie, Patricia had woken, but was quite distressed."

"May I ask why you needed Mrs Wright's help last night?" Asked Det. Insp. Clarke and then turned to Det. Sen. Const. Wallace, who she said would be taking notes and requiring a statement before they left.

"That's fine," I said as I sat reasonably relaxed beside Det. Insp. Clarke and began to explain to the two officers when I first realised something serious had occurred.

"When the young man, Kane, carried Patricia inside, I took her from him and realised she was in a worse state than I first thought."

"And what state did you think she would be in?" asked Det. Insp. Clarke, her large brown eyes studying every expression and movement I made.

"My first thought when I saw the kids on the porch, was that this could have been a prank. Patricia and her friend, Louise, like to muck around a lot. Then, I thought, she may have fallen on the dance floor or tripped over in the carpark on the way home. Later, when I felt blood and saw the scratches..."

"Now, back to my initial question, Michael." Det. Insp. Clarke asked, this time with less patience. "Why did you feel you needed Mrs Wright's help? You are a school teacher, are you not? Trained in First-Aid, and the management of adolescents."

I was slightly affronted by her suggestion that I may not be capable, after dedicating my whole working life to looking after children.

"I am a teacher, but I'm also realistic. I could tell this was a complex situation and it would be better if I had some sort of back-up." I answered truthfully and with words familiar to them.

"To my mind, there was a possibility that Patricia may have been assaulted, or worse." I paused, realising the devastation of either case.

"I thought it would be better for a mature woman, a mother and a social worker, to be with her if she needed to be changed or showered or other female things. It wouldn't be appropriate for me to do it — because Patricia's not my child — and I wouldn't do it anyway."

"Why not, Michael?" Det. Insp. Clarke asked with a further sign of doubt in her voice. She angled her chair to look at me more directly.

"Because there were accusations made against me at my previous school by a student." I hesitated and then added. "A female student."

"What were the accusations?" Det. Insp. Clarke asked in a clinical manner.

"Sexual assault."

Det. Sen. Const. Wallace leant over and then looked down the bench at me. Det. Insp. Clarke paused and then said.

"We were made aware of that incident earlier this morning … I'm glad you brought it up first."

I bet Andy couldn't wait to tell them. But how did he know about it?

"We immediately contacted your former principal, a Mr Ron Lewis."

"Yes, that's correct." I jumped in over Det. Insp. Clarke, who hid her annoyance well, and then continued.

"He confirmed that the matter had been thoroughly investigated by him and the local police and that you were completely exonerated. Is there anything else you would like to add to that?"

"It shook me up at the time … and still does. That's what I'd like to add — It could have finished my career — everything."

The officers spoke quietly to each other and then Det. Insp. Clarke returned to me.

"Has Patricia shown any signs of depression lately?

11

And we are aware teenagers can go through moody stages." Det. Insp. Clarke asked, taking a different tack in her inquiry, perhaps both officers realising I was being totally honest with them.

"No, not depressed, as such, but I know she misses her dad. She mentions him regularly."

"Michael, tell us about the last time you saw Patricia before she was carried back here." Det. Insp. Clarke said. A second before I could reply, Det. Sen. Const. Wallace asked if I could make him an instant coffee. Heather nodded as well. I went over and filled the kettle with water, and then pressed down on the small lever at the top.

"Okay, it was in the Sailing Club hall, about eleven, Pixie was…"

~

12

New Year's Eve, 1996. Late evening

Perspiration soaked the white frilly shirt of the cover band's lead singer as he swung his mic and black mullet hair around the cramped stage. Then with one arm raised as a fist to the sky, screamed out a more menacing version of *Devil Inside*, much to the appreciation of a hall packed with young people dancing and older people drinking.

As Michael stood watching the band, he felt an unexpected cold sensation on the exposed skin below his shorts. He looked immediately down to see a large hand pressing a can against his leg, then to the right to see Trev's boof-head and stubble-covered face smiling at him.

"Feel that, buddy boy. That's a cold can?"

Michael couldn't help but smile as Georgie, Roz and Jerry formed a tight circle around Trev so he could distribute to them either a cold beer can or West Coast Cooler from his ice-filled toolbox.

"Go on, have a swig. You'll like it." Trev said to Michael, squeezing Georgie close to him. "I knew the fridge would pack it in — I can't drink warm beer. And don't you go telling Steve or Jill, I've snuck some cold drinks in."

Michael looked over at the bar to see Steve step over and tap the beer fridge's thermostat with frustration, still wondering why it wasn't heading south, as Jill continued to serve a long line-up of revellers their lukewarm offerings.

"This heat must be a nightmare for Steve and Jill," Michael declared.

"Doesn't mean we have to suffer," Trev returned, grinning as he pulled out a beer can for himself from the slushy ice.

Michael looked over and could see a large group of girls, which included Pixie, Lou, and Isla, dancing together in the centre of the hall; a group of teenage boys stood nearby staring at them.

"I don't know how anybody could dance in here, it's like an oven and the band is as loud as…" Michael shouted as the band built to the climax of *Never Tear Us Apart*.

"To be quite honest, I'm not that big on New Year's Eve." Michael continued, "At least Christmas has something going for it. New Year's Eve is just another night."

"Don't be such a friggin' wet blanket, Michael.' Trev yelled back, "Everyone knows it's just an excuse to get pissed … If you've had a good year, you get pissed to celebrate. If you've had a shit year, you get pissed-er to commiserate."

"More pissed," Michael corrected, going over and tickling his adequate girth.

"Can't you teachers ever give up on correcting grammar?" Trev said as he slapped Michael's hand away.

Then, Georgie jumped in. "You say what you like, Michael. I'm just glad you and Fee met. We need more individuals around here. You're a breath of fresh air and don't forget it."

"Thanks, Georgie," Michael said through a surprised expression, stepping back to give her a small bow. Jerry and Roz raised their eyebrows at a rare show of independence against Trev's overbearing demeanour.

Shortly afterwards Georgie said to her husband "About time you asked me to dance, isn't it?" while grabbing Trev by the arm and dragging him out onto the dance floor,

"Well, come on, hurry up."

"I tell ya, the band's earning their dough, tonight." Michael said returning to face Jerry and Roz, "It's been as hot as Hades in that corner of the hall all day and the lead singer's not holding back on his moves, either."

"They're good," Jerry said. "Real professionals. The club needed a band that wasn't going to pull the pin as soon as the mercury hit the ton."

Roz then changed the direction of the conversation.

"Are you looking forward to the challenge at the Girls' Secondary?" she asked, genuinely interested. "You have big shoes to fill."

"I certainly do. I'll approach things very low key. Stick to the basics. It must have been such a huge loss for the school to lose Mrs Craig so quickly. I believe she was much loved by both students and teachers."

"Yes, she was, and it *was* way too quick," Roz said quite despondently, obvious that she knew her well.

"Jillian was Trace's favourite teacher. She could call her up on any night of the week if she was stuck on something. Jillian would stay on the line no matter how long until Trace worked it out."

Michael felt a large degree of embarrassment that his opportunity to work closer to Fiona's home had come on the back of a personal tragedy. A wave of exhaustion then washed over him, brought about by several nights with little sleep. He made a decision.

"You know what. I might pull the pin, myself." Michael exclaimed, having resolved it was the wisest thing to do,

"Nothing against you guys, but I'm actually knackered. Zac's already gone and Pixie's got Lou sleeping over, so they'll head home together. I might as well take off now."

"No problems, mate." Jerry said, not concerned with Michael exiting, "We're suckers to sing the song, so we'll stick around for that. But before you go — Happy New Year."

"Thanks, mate, Happy New Year," Michael said as he shook Jerry's hand. "And a Happy New Year to you, too, Roz." then kissed her on the cheek.

Roz then said sincerely. "I hope you and Fee have a wonderful year — Okay."

"Likewise." Michael shouted as he began to push through the bustle of the crowd, not wanting to prolong his goodbye, "See you later."

Making his way towards the carpark exit, Michael caught a glimpse of Jill and Steve as they continued to be run off their feet behind the bar, and wondered at their amazing loyalty and commitment to this club.

As Michael reached the door, he took a final look behind him. On the opposite side of the hall, he could see Tracey standing alone near the access road door staring in the direction of Pixie, Lou, and their large group of friends dancing in front of the band.

Michael satisfied that there was no reason for him to stay, exited by the carpark stairs and then walked towards home.

~

13

New Year's Day, 1997. Afternoon

Det. Insp. Clarke swallowed down the last drop of her coffee, placed the cup gently on the bench and then asked; her eyes fixed on mine.

"So you came straight back here, Michael?"

"I did. I had a quick beer, a cold beer, to help me sleep, then hit the sack a good twenty minutes before midnight ... I can vaguely recall seeing flashes of light and hearing fireworks go off, as well as something like Auld Lang Syne being sung ... but I couldn't be sure."

The two police officers restless after their recent shots of caffeine straightened on their chairs.

"Almost finished ... for the moment." Det. Insp. Clarke said and then paused to perhaps give more emphasis to what she was about to say.

"Now, I'm sure you're keen to get to the hospital to support Patricia and Mrs Farnes, but there are some personal matters concerning Patricia that I would like to discuss."

"Sure," I replied not afraid to answer any question that would help the police catch the people responsible for drugging her, while also realising that my contact with Fiona's daughter had been limited over the year and there was no guarantee that the personal matters she had thrust upon me — were even true.

"Fire away."

"Okay, has Patricia confided in you about any relationships she has had, or is having? Boyfriends, boys she hangs around with or talks about a lot; anything that might be distressing her in that part of her life? If there is, we need to know about it."

I wasn't immediately comfortable with this question. Relationships between teenagers were by nature brief and all over the place and were unlikely to end up with a kid being drugged or assaulted.

I stood, not convinced Heather was on the right track with her inquiry. Then with Det. Sen. Const. Wallace following my every move, I walked over to the nearest venetian blind to let in more light.

"I'm a bit confused here," I said as I turned back to face the detectives. "I've seen plenty of breakups between teens and they rarely go past a few tears and a few weeks."

"To me, this is something different."

"I didn't want to go into any specifics unless I had to,"

replied Det. Insp. Clarke, somewhat annoyed at having to justify her questioning.

"But, there has been a pattern developing over the last couple of years … And that is of school kids getting their hands on date-rape drugs and using them for all types of reasons; revenge, targeting the person they want, whatever … but there's a new drug on the block called *GHB*. It's powerful and its side-effects are unpredictable."

"What I'm asking for, is any piece of information that will help us catch the people supplying teens with this drug before we have any more fatalities."

"More fatalities?" I queried, ignorant of the fact, especially as a teacher, that there had been any deaths from date-rape drugs.

"Absolutely, the state is awash with drugs of every description at the moment, but this is an extremely bad one. So your help with any relevant information would be greatly appreciated — and as you are aware, you have certain obligations as a teacher."

~

14

New Year's Day, 1997. Late afternoon

Each step echoed as I walked nervously down the long and quiet corridor towards Ward 4 AMU of the Alfred Hospital. The frosty way Fiona and my phone conversation had ended late last night again weighing heavily on my mind.

What also dominated my thoughts was what Fiona may have been told between then and now by her ex-husband. I had to believe our relationship was strong enough to withstand anything. But *this* wasn't just anything.

The corridor emptied into a sterile and empty waiting room; a nurses' station stood close by automated doors situated to the right of the area. Tired green eyes peered over a wide, curved desk and seemed to sum me up, and down, as I approached.

"Can I help you?" a woman of around fifty years of

age asked clinically, as she sat upright in her perfectly starched and ironed light blue nurses' uniform.

"Hi!" I answered cheerfully in contrast. "I'm here to check on the welfare of Patricia Farnes. I'm also hoping to see her mother, Fiona. My name is Michael Freeman."

The nurse, who I assumed was not happy to be working New Year's Day, then looked over a broadsheet on her desk and replied with a little more enthusiasm.

"Pixie, of course. She only arrived here a short time ago. Are you a relative?" asked the nurse, whose name read as SRN Marg King on her identification tag.

"No, I'm Mrs Farnes' partner."

Nurse King again looked warily at me, the word 'partner' sometimes producing a guarded response.

"Take a seat, Michael. I'll make a call."

I had no trouble finding a seat amongst the dozen laid out in two equal rows opposite the nurses' station. Nurse King's call didn't happen as soon as I expected, although, I did understand my needs were far from priority around here.

Within a minute of Nurse King making a call, the automated doors slid open. Fiona stepped through the opening, looked around expectantly, and then spotted me in readiness to greet her.

"Oh, Michael," Fiona said as she rushed over and forced her arms around me. She kissed the side of my face, her tears running down my cheek.

"I was so frightened when I got your call last night. I think I'm going to lose Pixie every day — I really do."

I was immediately troubled by Fiona's comment. It wasn't healthy for her to be in constant fear for her daughter's welfare, for no logical reason. Nevertheless, Fiona was happy to be in my arms, and I was relieved to have her there.

"Pixie's strong, Fee," I assured as we gradually released from each other. "You know that. She's safe now."

"I know, but Andy and my break-up was so hard on her. I've always worried that something like this would happen."

A distraught Fiona took me by the hand and led me away from the nurses' station.

"Are you alright, Fee? What have the doctors told you?" I asked, concerned now for her emotional state.

"They said to me when I first arrived." Fiona then fought hard to compose herself.

"'Patricia has suffered a trauma … No specific interference or foreign substances have been noted. We don't believe Patricia has been violated.'"

At arm's length, I held tightly onto Fiona's shaking hands.

"Their exact fucking words," she added.

My eyes glazed over and I felt gutted for Fiona to have to hear that about her daughter.

"What the hell did they mean by that?"

"I know what…" Fiona said as she wiped tears from her face, "She was lucky … lucky she hadn't been raped."

I'll kill the bastards who did this.

~

Through the automated doors, Zac strolled out as nonchalantly as ever. He saw us and then walked slowly over.

"Hi, Michael," he said in his not quite broken voice and then spoke directly to his mother.

"Mum, can you come and talk to Pix, please. She keeps going on and on about wanting to go home. She's giving me the irrates."

Some things don't change.

Fiona seemed to acknowledge my thoughts and gave me a tiny smile.

"Try to remember why we're here, love," Fiona said rubbing Zac's shoulder. "And just put up with it for a while. Can you — please?"

Zac rolled his eyes with reluctant acceptance and then strolled back through the automated doors.

"Please come in," Fiona asked genuinely and then added in a happier tone.

"Pix did ask only twenty minutes ago when you were coming in. She does want to see you … Nurse Ratched said it was okay if you stayed for a short time."

"Okay, if you're sure that's alright," I replied and then thought I should ask about another subject.

"Have you spoken to Andy?" Dreading the thought of how much he would have embellished the accusations made against me by a schoolgirl named Linda.

Fiona whispered. "Not before I spoke to Roz ... Of course, Andy shit-stirred as much as he could about the schoolgirl's photos, which he couldn't wait to tell me about. It was a bit of a shock to hear it, though."

"I should have told you about the allegations made against me," I said as a sincere apology.

"You should have..." Fiona replied with understandable annoyance. "Luckily I had Roz around to explain to me in great detail about their scheming. In the end, I was *so* glad when Andy went home."

"Did Roz also tell you that Pixie scratched my arm and screamed out my name before we left for the hospital?" I asked wanting to be up-front with Fiona as much as possible without overwhelming her.

"I'm completely lost for why she would do that." I added, "It was like she was trying to break away from someone."

Fiona then withdrew into herself, perhaps imagining the fear her daughter would have gone through less than sixteen hours earlier and then just as quickly returned to the present and me.

"Can we leave that for now, Michael … Let's go in," Fiona said as she again grabbed my hand.

~

Within an enclosure, only a short distance inside Ward 4, Pixie sat upright in an Acute Assessment bed as an oxygen mask was being strapped over her nose and mouth by a young nurse; the nurse then began to wrap the cuff of a blood pressure monitor around Pixie's left arm. Under soft artificial light, Zac sat quietly reading a magazine on a metal-framed chair in the far corner.

Pixie gave a small wave to her mum as she re-entered the enclosure, and then as her eyes fell upon me, pulled her oxygen mask down and said in a flat, unwelcoming tone, which echoed throughout the ward.

"Michael!"

I froze to the spot, unsure what I had done, then looked to Fiona for guidance, but she opened out her hands to indicate she had no explanation. I turned back to Pixie and the nurse who had given up on her attempt to take an observation and released the pressure off the cuff.

"Pixie, I don't have to stay if you don't want me to. I just wanted to say a quick hello."

If I'd only stayed at the club until midnight.

"No!" Pixie exclaimed. "It's him."

The nurse studied Pixie's wide-eyed expression and then asked.

"Would you like some water, Pixie?"

Pixie shook her head abruptly from side to side and then yelled a blatant, "No!"

The young nurse then tried to replace the oxygen mask over Pixie's nose and mouth, but with no success; she then turned to all others in the enclosure and said calmly.

"I might get everyone to leave for a moment if you don't mind."

As Zac, Fiona, and I prepared to leave as one, Pixie ripped the mask completely off her face.

"No, Mum, stay!" she screamed. "It's his name. The boy that gave me the Coke and grabbed my arm."

"His name's Michael."

I closed my eyes and breathed in deeply, and even though this would be bringing back harrowing memories of a disgusting young man, it was important for Pixie to remember everything, no matter how traumatic.

As she hugged her daughter, Fiona looked over at me with a determination on her face that said.

We will get them.

~

15

Friday, 3rd January 1997. Late morning

From the master bedroom, the sky above Beaumaris had taken on a slate grey appearance. On the horizon, heavy rain clouds rolled in and a freshening wind swirled dust and leaves around the street below. I searched up and down the rows of houses for a familiar face, not having seen a neighbour since leaving for the Alfred Hospital on New Year's Day.

I suspected that Fiona's friends, now aware of the seriousness of the incident that had put Pixie in hospital, had decided to give Fiona and her family the space necessary to settle back into some sort of normality, and would gradually drop in to visit once an acceptable time had passed. The only guarantee was a visit from Andy once Pixie returned home.

My attention was then drawn to the white duco and blue light of a police divisional van pulling up in front of Roz and Jerry's home. Det. Insp. Clarke and Det. Sen. Const. Wallace exited the vehicle. As they took their first steps they looked up at me standing in the frame of the master bedroom window.

Not again.

Half expecting the detectives to walk towards our drive, I was surprised when they went into the property that their vehicle stood in front of.

Fiona, who had snuck up behind me and placed an arm gently over my shoulder, watched as they proceeded up next door's driveway, then said with the ease of a mother who had been informed an hour earlier that her daughter had been cleared to return home tomorrow.

"They're back," Although, showing no interest in why.

"Yeah…" I agreed, but not quite as unconcerned as Fiona.

"I'm a bit unsure why they've come back," I said. "Everyone who was involved on the night has given a statement and I saw the police having a look around the Sailing Club carpark and on the beach."

Fiona was unresponsive.

"Maybe, they've found the guys," I continued. "Maybe, they want Tracey to go through a few mug shots — Do they even do mug shots anymore?

"I'm pretty sure they do." Fiona said tugging at my shoulder to make me leave the window, "All I know is

Pixie's coming home tomorrow. She's in a great frame of mind and wants to put all of this behind her."

"She could put it behind her a lot quicker if the cops searched for those guys somewhere else instead of here."

"Michael, they're just doing their job," Fiona said as she took my hand to lead me towards the stairs. "And how crazy was it that one of those shits was called Michael."

"Yeah, that sort of stuff can get you hanged," I replied scratching my head at how easily things can appear different to how they are.

"You know, I really thought Pixie was screaming at me in her bedroom before we left for the hospital ... Roz gave me a real funny look about that."

"I bet she did," Fiona said kissing my cheek. "Look, as far as Pixie's concerned, she can't believe she took a drink from guys like that in a carpark, whether she'd met them before or not ... Although, she swears it was a new bottle of Coke."

"Clever shits, aren't they?"

"Things will calm down," Fiona said as we headed down the hallway, stopping outside Pixie's room. "They have to."

She then asked while pushing open the door.

"Can you help me put some new sheets on Pix's bed?"

~

Fiona called to me from the hallway just as I was on the point of dozing off on the couch in the family room. She asked me to come quickly to look at something. Seconds later, I found her in the foyer, staring through the narrow glass panels of the front door.

"Michael, have a look at this. Something's not right with Lou."

I moved beside Fiona, leant down and had a look for myself. Lou was standing on the opposite side of the road on the nature strip in front of her home, in drizzling rain, dressed in only jeans and a tee-shirt, while staring at Roz and Jerry's house.

"That is definitely not right, Fee," I said and wondered if I had underestimated how much New Year's Eve had affected Lou.

"Lou's a funny kid, sometimes." Fiona said, "So happy-go-lucky one minute then takes everything to heart, the next."

To make sure she wasn't overstating the situation, Fiona again looked through the window.

"Standing in the rain is certainly not a smart thing to do on any day." She added.

"I'll go and talk to Lou," I said, although hesitant after my poor behaviour towards her at the hospital. Fiona shook her head.

"No, I should go. I've known Lou for a long time."

Fiona grabbed her raincoat from the stand, gave me

a smile as she pulled the hood over her head and then left in a rush through the front door and off the porch. Shortly afterwards, Fiona stood in front of Lou, not allowing her to look at the house across the road. She offered and soon had Lou wrapped in her arms, at the same time as the drizzle turned to steady rain.

An animated conversation took place between Fiona and Lou, followed a minute later with Lou nodding her head, separating from Fiona, and then running through puddles towards the front door of her home.

I had stepped out onto the porch to get a better view of proceedings and waited for Fiona with a thick towel in hand as she stepped cautiously through a sheet of water running down the street. Out of next door's drive, my attention was drawn again to Det. Insp. Clarke and her off-sider, Det. Sen. Const. Wallace, as they raced towards their divisional van. After diving inside they quickly activated windscreen wipers and then drove off towards Beach Road.

Fiona turned from watching the divisional van leave and then stepped up onto our porch, immediately strip-ping off her raincoat. I passed Fiona the towel.

"See, Michael. They didn't stay long."

However, I was more concerned with what was going on in Lou's mind, than what the police were up to.

"Is Lou alright?"

"I'm not sure how to answer that," Fiona said, carrying her raincoat to the end of the porch and shaking it.

"She kept on repeating, 'Why can't anybody see what's going on?' I asked her what she meant by that, but she wouldn't say. I wasn't sure what else I could do, except say everything will be alright. Just give it time."

"It has to have something to do with New Year's Eve, don't you think?" I said to Fiona who shook my statement off just as quickly as the water from her coat.

Before we could return inside out of the cold breeze, Roz appeared unexpectedly, running up the small steps from our driveway, and then flew up the stairs onto our porch. Jerry followed closely behind. Not a smile between them.

"Hi, neighbours," Fiona said, welcoming them cheerfully. "The cops forget something?"

"You could say that..." Roz said coldly as Jerry put an arm around her; their demeanour incredibly negative.

"Bit of a miserable day, isn't it?" I said with optimism while suspecting that not only the weather but the conversation was about to turn sour.

"A bloody miserable day for our daughter," Roz said, before placing a hand over her mouth.

"Tell me what's wrong, Roz." Fiona said trying to calm her, "Come inside and we'll talk about it."

"I'm not going inside with that — man." She replied angrily.

I took a step back in shock from the aggressive nature of Roz's words. Fiona gave me a sideways look.

"Do you know what this is about, Michael?" Fiona asked quietly as if this could only be a misunderstanding, then before I could begin to explain, Roz spoke to Fiona as if I wasn't there.

"You ask him Fee if he said something to the police about Trace."

Fiona turned her eyes towards me again.

"What did you tell the police, Michael?" Fiona asked, perhaps without fully understanding how destructive this conversation had become.

"I answered the questions that the police asked me, Fee, and that is something I shouldn't have to discuss on a wet porch."

Roz cut in, not letting up on me.

"Not when it involves our daughter. You think Trace is responsible for this — Don't you?"

I replied abruptly. "Don't accuse me of anything, except trying to find out who hurt Pixie."

Fiona looked around confused. "Wait, wait — I can't take this in. I'm not part of the conversation — Who hurt Pixie?"

"Ask Michael," Jerry said bitterly to Fiona. "He's already made up his mind who did it."

Jerry took a step towards me. I held my ground. There was no reason I shouldn't. Fiona then quickly stepped in between us to prevent an ugly scene and pleaded.

"Can we please take this inside?"

Roz and Jerry reluctantly nodded their heads in agreement, shuffling closely past Fiona as they went through the front door.

~

Roz and Jerry entered the family room, immediately refusing Fiona's offer to sit at the kitchen bench; too agitated other than to stand and glare at me.

Roz couldn't wait to bring up something I had already been upfront with her about.

"Did you happen to mention to Fiona about the accusation of assault made against you by a female student?" Roz asked as if it was up to her when I did so.

"Well ... have you?"

"Of course, I have, Roz. Anyway, I know you went through it with Fee at the hospital. The police contacted my principal. He confirmed the girls had made it up. So, I won't be taking any shit about that."

"Nothing happened."

"Teachers do get targeted, Roz," Fiona said in a conciliatory manner.

Roz turned away, frustrated that I wouldn't admit to something I hadn't done. Jerry again took her into his arms.

"We're not here about that," Jerry said, his appearance strained as he looked at Fiona. "The police wanted to talk to Tracey on her own about information they've gathered recently ... They wanted to ask Trace about the nature of her relationship with Pixie."

Jerry then looked directly at me. I believed I knew the reason.

"Tracey was too upset to say a lot after they left, but we're almost certain someone the police would take seriously and who was there on the night, has suggested Trace was involved in what happened to Pixie."

"There's no way Trace would hurt Pix," Fiona responded strongly, bewildered by what she had heard, then looked at Jerry and Roz in turn and said. "We know that's not possible."

"Michael, do you know anything about this?" Fiona asked, leaning forward, her mouth open, willing me to say the words, 'No, I don't.'

But, I couldn't, because I did know. Although, I wished I had never got up to investigate a noise on a hot and still night.

Roz stepped beside Fiona and then demanded.

"If you know something, Michael, you should tell us."

I had been pushed into a corner. There was no other way out except through honesty.

"I do know what Roz and Jerry are talking about, Fee," I said quietly, even though this kangaroo court had arrived before I had a chance to explain, in a rational way, and only with Fiona, the complexity of what had happened while she was away.

"But, it is definitely not the right time or place to discuss this ... Fee, can I speak to you alone?"

This time Fiona glared at me as she leant forward and then said emphatically.

"Michael, can you please tell me — now."

I lowered my head, unable to look at the pain on Fiona's face and then spoke to her as gently as I could.

"Fee ... Pix has told me things over the past few months. I told her I didn't want to know about them, but she told me anyway."

I paused, but it had to be said.

"Pixie told me that she and Tracey had experimented ... a couple of years back."

"So what, that's growing up!" Jerry shouted. "No need to blab to the police about it."

I wasn't going to back down to Jerry or Roz's brow-beating, it was about time they started accepting some responsibility for their daughter's behaviour.

Fiona spoke quietly to me. "Michael, you know that's nothing."

"Fee..." I paused for as long as my conscience would allow, before crossing a line that I could never return over.

"I also caught Zac and Tracey together."

The room fell silent, mouths agape before Fiona gasped, the look she then gave me as a betrayer, broke my heart. Roz put her arms around her, but Fiona was unmoved by the gesture. Jerry rocked his tall frame from side to side in shock and then sneered through clenched teeth.

"That's a lie."

I had to go the course, to stop now would be betraying myself. I replied as clearly and deliberately as I could.

"I'm sorry, Jerry ... It's not."

Fiona pushed gently away from Roz and then stood toe to toe with me.

"You could have told me this before now, Michael. Hasn't my family suffered enough?"

"Fee, these were confidences, at the time, which weren't mine to break."

"So," Jerry mocked from behind. "It was easier to confide in the police, you weak bastard than to tell their *bloody parents!*"

Fiona then threw her hands up into the air as if in exasperation and walked away from everyone, stopping at the back door to open it. She held it open to allow cold air to stream in and over her face; pretending to study the shimmer of light rain on the surface of the pool.

Fiona then turned slowly back to face us.

"This is a shock for everyone," She said, her voice fading, then briefly held her breath before continuing. "So perhaps we should take a step back and reflect on what this means for our children ... That would probably be for the best."

Roz whispered something to Jerry and then spoke to Fiona.

"Tracey's on her own, Fee. We should get back to her."

However, Fiona was only half-listening, her face drawn as she stood in a daze. I wanted to rush over and comfort her, to tell her I loved her, to tell her that after I explain, everything would be alright and return to normal; but I was fooling myself — it was already too late.

Fiona's eyes were on Roz as she tapped Jerry on the shoulder to hurry him to leave when they suddenly shifted to the hallway entrance, and Zac, who had just come through it.

"I could hear Trace's name. Is she okay?" asked a heavy-eyed teen, whose lack of sleep had finally caught up with him.

"Trace is fine, love ... She's fine." Fiona answered ahead of Roz, opening up her arms as she strode over to hug her son, adding softly when she arrived,

"Zac, we need to talk about something."

Fiona looked over at Jerry and Roz, who were unsure in which direction to look or move, and then asked without a hint of anger in her voice.

"Can I please be alone with Zac?"

After a few seconds, Fiona turned to me.

"And that includes you, Michael."

I wasn't devastated. I understood. To tell the truth has its consequences.

I accepted Fiona's wishes without argument and then left for the master bedroom, unable to meet the eyes of those around me.

Halfway down the hall I stopped and called back to a room full of hushed voices.

"I'll pack some things."

I didn't wait for a response, only sprinted upstairs to find a bag.

~

PART THREE
UNWELCOME HOME

1

On the old boat ramp below Beach Road, a couple of metres from the walking path on Mentone Beach, I gazed at the progress of a large grey cloud and the rain it was releasing. This blight on an otherwise blue sky moved across a calm Beaumaris Bay in my general direction. The wind picked up and I welcomed the freshness on my face and arms.

I needed it to wake me from the lethargy and despondency I had fallen into over the preceding weeks, and even though my relationship with Fiona had taken tentative steps towards a new start, and hopefully in turn with the rest of her family, I also wanted to mend other relationships before I could move forward.

I eagerly awaited the return of Tracey from her regular walk.

A quarter of an hour later, Tracey, with her eyes also

fixed on the approaching rain, turned and headed up the ramp. As she straightened, she caught sight of me through a light drizzle. She stopped suddenly and then looked back at the walking path as if contemplating a return; saying something under her breath she continued on until she stood before me.

"Hi, Tracey," I said with trepidation, knowing this might be a horrible mistake to try to fix the unfixable. Nevertheless, I continued.

"Have a good walk?"

"It was good, thanks," Tracey replied with the politeness she had always used and then added in a rush. "Let's get under the shelter. We're going to get soaked in a second."

Walking at a brisk rate we descended the ramp and then stepped over the path wall, grains of sand stinging the backs of our legs as we turned our faces away from the wind under the vacant picnic shelter.

"It makes you feel alive this rain. Doesn't it?" Tracey said, holding her ground close to me.

"It does," I replied, finding a small taste of wintry freshness exhilarating after weeks of persistent heat.

"Can we talk?" I asked. "I would completely understand if you didn't want to."

Tracey looked at me sideways, as if weighing up my sincerity and then replied.

"No-one has said I couldn't, or shouldn't. I'm sure it

can't be as bad as the dressing-downs I've had over the last few weeks from the police, half a dozen welfare workers and my parents — I'm sure I can take anything *you* have to say."

"As long as it's not about Zac. I don't even know what that was about." Tracey said before she may have thought that comment sounded a bit selfish, "Sorry, how is Zac?"

"Fine, I think." I replied, glad she had given him some acknowledgement, "I haven't seen him in a while, but you know how resilient he is."

I ummed and ahhed not sure what to say next which allowed Tracey to get in first.

"For a start, you're an arsehole for dobbing me in to the police."

There was little I could say in response … and how was it possible to apologise for an ill-thought-out decision.

"Tracey, can I…"

"Shut up, Michael. I don't want to hear excuses."

Tracey lifted the hood of her windcheater and then placed it over her head.

I knew this would happen.

"You're right, I probably deserve silence … I'd better go."

Tracey turned sharply to face me. "Stop being a drama queen, Michael — All you did was put Pixie and her family first."

Tracey then faced the breeze and looked across the

bay, the sun beginning to break through the dissipating cloud as the rain eased and the wind began to abate.

"You know, a friend of mine who moved to the Grammar from Frankston High a while back, told me about you. Lou knows her. She reckons you were cool with the kids. They had a lot of respect for you. She also told me about the photos that went around the school."

"Those photos nearly sent me to the looney bin."

Tracey nodded her head in reply.

"She also said there was another shit story that went around, about you leaving your wife when she became ill and not bothering to visit her in hospital."

I suggested we go and sit on the volcanic rock that formed a low wall at the side of the ramp while contemplating why people felt the need to perpetuate sick rumours and plain untruths.

"I haven't heard that one for a while," I responded barely loud enough for Tracey to hear, annoyed that another story I had thought buried, had returned to haunt.

"Can I tell you my version of the truth — or — what actually happened?"

Tracey nodded again.

"For a start, my ex became sick *well after* we divorced, and her illness had nothing at all to do with our separation. The first time I went to visit her in hospital, her brother was drunk and wanted to fight. So, to avoid any crap, I arranged with the Nurse Manager to visit after hours. Six months later. Thank God. She was given the all-clear."

"Alright, you're a bloody saint," Tracey said and then produced the beginnings of a smile. "And just so you know, I didn't lie about New Year's Eve. I wouldn't do that."

She then said quietly. "But I did leave things out."

"I thought some detail was missing," I said in reply, but at the same time wondering why Tracey had even mentioned New Year's Eve.

Tracey then looked down at her feet as she spoke.

"I've been trying to build up the courage to tell Mum and Dad about what really happened that night, but I can't hurt them any more than I already have. I can't tell them what that makes me … besides other things."

"Your parents are caring people, Tracey," I said, assuming more than I should. "They love you and *will* understand."

"I know, but I've felt so alone over the last few years. I can't believe it myself at times."

I sensed Tracey wanted to say more. I had to assure her that I could keep a confidence — this time.

"If you want to talk. It won't go over the road." I told Tracey, holding my gaze on the side of her face. "It wouldn't have, anyway."

"What do you want to do?" I asked quietly.

"I want to tell *someone* what happened New Year's Eve," Tracey replied in a whisper.

"Then you can…"

Tracey's eyes were on mine until she was convinced that I was nothing more than genuine. She began slowly.

"You probably know some of this, but after you left the club, most people were up dancing. Lou, Pixie, and a few of their mates were dancing in front of the band. Kane and his bunch of nerds were hanging around nearby. Pixie went to get a drink at the bar. There were about six or seven people in front of her … Guess who came up and stood behind her?"

"Kane."

"Of course the pathetic shit did," Tracey said and was happy to go on.

"Kane tapped Pixie on the shoulder. She spun around so fast I swear she was going to slap his friggin' face. He's such a bloody pest."

"Pixie was about to lose it, but instead, pushed him out of the way and went outside by the carpark door, probably to calm herself down. Kane went sooking back to his mates."

"Did you go outside to see what Pixie was up to?"

"Not straight away … I'm not all smitten like Kane."

I resisted an urge to ask about something that was becoming all too obvious.

"When I got outside, I stood out of sight near the top of the stairs and could see Pixie leaning against the bonnet of a white panel van, talking to two guys with bleached hair. I'm sure I've seen them somewhere before. The shorter one strutted about like he was it and a bit. The taller one had a bottle in his hand, probably Coke."

"The tall surfie passed the bottle to Pixie, who had to twist hard to take the top off. It fizzed like a new bottle would. After it stopped fizzing she took a long swig and then another."

"Nobody would have suspected it was spiked," I added bitterly.

"Everything seemed okay until the tall surfie tried to put his arm around her. Straight off, Pix pulled away and told him to piss off. That's when he turned nasty. He grabbed Pixie by the arm and called her a 'skinny stuck-up bitch.' — She looked so frightened."

Tracey's expression showed the strain as she seemed to re-run the events through her mind.

"There were lots of people around, screaming and carrying on. I suppose that's why nobody seemed to take any notice of her yelling. I was glad when Kane came up the road on the other side of the club. I expected him to race over and take on these guys."

"But instead, he just stood there like a zombie, watching Pixie being yelled at by that bastard — Then he disappeared like a chicken-shit."

"I had to do something, no-one else was, so I got up to the top of the stairs and ran flat out at the white-haired prick. When I got to him, I tried to pull his hand off

Pixie's arm, but he was too strong. Before I knew it his thug of a mate had his arm around my neck and threw me to the ground like I was nothing."

Why didn't Tracey tell us she'd taken on these guys?

"I was about to run back inside to get help when Pixie screamed out something and dug her nails into the prick's arm ... He let go and she then ran down the road on the far side of the clubrooms. Both the pricks got into their van, I presume to drive off. I'm not sure if they did because I was already half-way down the carpark stairs. I wanted to get back inside to make sure Pixie was alright."

Tracey closed her eyes and tried to control her rapid breathing. I gave her time to regain her composure.

"Pixie scratches well," I said eventually, showing Tracey the nail marks still evident on my arm, but I may as well have spoken to the bitumen path.

Tracey and I sat for a few moments in silence. I was shocked that Kane had left Pixie when she needed him and that Tracey had taken on these guys, and then wondered why Kane had not at least gone to get help — perhaps he had been too embarrassed for running away.

"It must have been a harrowing experience for both you and Pixie," I stated.

"It was," Tracey replied quietly. "But the weirdest thing was, when I got back inside I saw Kane lined up to get a drink as if nothing had happened. I also expected to see

Pixie going on to Lou about the fight with the surfies …
but Pixie wasn't even in the hall."

"If the Coke was spiked, it might have already hit her
hard," I said in response. "She mightn't have known
where she was."

"I thought the Coke might have had something in it,"
Tracey said, rubbing her arm, perhaps remembering
where she fell. "That's why I went outside to look for her."

Tracey then stopped rubbing her arm.

"You know, I would never dob Kane in for shitting
himself. I nearly did myself, and I know he's on his last
warning at the Grammar for taking a swing at a teacher
— Apparently he was stoned at the time." Tracey said,
only keeping her annoyance at him down because an
older couple were walking past us towards the beach.

"But, what pissed me off more was Lou, dancing away
with her cliquey mates. In the whole time, she never
wondered where her best friend was." Tracey said turning again to face me.

"I know why — because she was too busy cracking
onto boys to think about anyone else."

I saw a tear run down the side of Tracey's face and
thought I should offer her a break so she could calm
herself.

"Maybe, we should talk about this another time." I
suggested, "I can meet you here again tomorrow."

I went to stand but Tracey grabbed the back of my

tee-shirt preventing me from moving, "Where are you going?" She asked, and then said. "Let me get this done now, Michael … Because after today, for my own sanity, I have to let it go."

The relieved expression on Tracey's face as I sat back down showed me she needed to continue, to free herself of the massive burden the last few months had produced.

Having accepted she wanted to continue, I asked, only to confirm.

"Do you mind if I ask you something *very* personal? It's about you and Pixie." Tracey stood immediately and began to walk down the ramp, then onto the walking path.

I should have left it alone.

Then, Tracey turned and shouted. "Come on. I'll show you where I found Pix."

~

I caught up to Tracey thirty metres from the Sailing Club on our way towards the cliffs.

"Okay," Tracey said, without a hint of uncertainty. "Ask away."

I hesitated before I said. "Do you like Pixie — a lot?"

Silence followed my question as three elderly members of the Icebergers ran across our path on their way to the glistening water. After passing the clubrooms, Tracey replied clearly.

"You know I do — but I wish the hell I didn't."

We continued two hundred metres further on until we stopped opposite a roughly hacked-back melaleuca bush.

"That's it, that's where I found Pixie," Tracey said, pointing to a spot on the sand beside the bush.

~

2

New Year's Eve, 1996. Close to midnight

There was a time when Pixie followed me … it wasn't that long ago.

I could see a girl walking unsteadily as she negotiated a sweeping bend along the dimly lit path from the Sailing Club to the cliffs of Beaumaris Bay; the girl's blonde hair clearly visible as fireworks began to burst around the bay signalling the end of one year and the beginning of another.

It has to be Pixie.

From the main hall of the clubrooms, the band and crowd began to count down the last thirty seconds of Nineteen-ninety-six.

Cries of 'Happy New Year' went up at the same time as I saw the silhouette of the girl stagger off the path onto the sand beside a bush shrouded in grey. Bending down low the figure appeared to retch onto the sand. After standing, she looked around unsure of what all the yelling and singing was about.

The girl was then lost from my sight as she moved further away from the path.

~

I arrived beside the melaleuca bush to see the girl, partially illuminated by fireworks, crouched in preparation to have a pee.

"Pixie, is that you?" I asked quietly. "Are you alright?"

"Jesus, bloody Christ, Tracey!" Pixie slurred, her eyes barely open as she forced herself to stand.

"Does a bell go off in your twot when a kid pulls their undies down?"

"I'm just checking up on you Pix." I replied, resisting the urge to scream back at her, "There's no need to be a bitch. Do you want me to grab Lou?"

"No, I want you to fuck off!" Pixie shouted.

I controlled my anger, telling myself 'it's the drugs talking, it's the drugs, not Pixie'.

"Well, I'm not. Those two guys that gave you the Coke have drugged you. They could have put any shit in that bottle. You need to go back to the clubrooms."

Pixie waved me away as she lurched from side to side. I needed to find words strong enough to make her understand the danger she had put herself in.

"They wanted to rape you, Pix — Get that? — Rape you!"

"Stop bloody talking will you. You stupid bitch." Pixie yelled as she staggered forward barely able to maintain her footing.

"Okay, I'll give you what you want."

Pixie searched for the hem of her dress and then lifted it, revealing herself to me. I shuddered as I averted my eyes, realising how pathetic Pixie must think I was.

"That's what you wanted to see — Wasn't it?" Pixie sneered.

"Now leave me and Zac alone or I'll call the fucking police on you."

I broke down and began to cry. "Pix, I'm sorry..." I murmured and then walked away from her towards the cliffs; fireworks burst sporadically along the way to light a path.

We grew up together, Pix — How could you ever forget that?

~

3

....

Saturday, 22nd February 1997. Mid-morning

Tracey covered her face with her hands, and then wiped tears away from her cheeks. We then stood and stared at a neglected, but otherwise inconsequential melaleuca bush.

"Did you go all the way to the cliffs?" I asked, understanding the need for Tracey to finish the story.

"No," Tracey said as she looked towards the ancient bluff, "I sat on a stormwater drain down there." Pointing to the middle pipe of three that protruded from the lower section of the beach.

"I was only there for a few minutes when I heard a squeal. It sounded like Pixie and came from around here — I wanted to walk away. I really didn't want to go back."

"...but you did."

"Yes, I ran back — and if those surfie bastards had've been there. I would have fuckin' killed 'em." Tracey shouted, releasing a torrent of pent up anger that must have been held in since New Year.

Tracey then slowly leant down and grabbed a handful of sand from just off the path, and let it slowly drain through her fingers.

"No-one can know what I told you, Michael — No-one!"

"They won't," I said and then gave Tracey time before I asked one final question,

"Did you see anyone hanging around here — Anyone at all?"

"I thought I saw someone running up the small path to the carpark … I couldn't be sure," Tracey said as she turned to point out the path, almost overgrown with ti-tree,

"Outside the clubrooms, lots of people were talking and laughing. I could see Lou in the distance walk this way. As she got closer she called out Pixie's name."

Tracey then said quietly as she wiped the last of the sand from her fingers. "I should have gone earlier and got help from Mum and Dad in the clubrooms … It's obvious now."

I needed to say something to Tracey to stop her from blaming herself.

"You did the right thing to follow Pixie. You were the only one who kept an eye on her — You probably scared off the attacker."

Tracey went quiet, appearing to digest and hopefully accept what I had said.

"Lou looked at me strangely when she arrived here. Kane turned up a couple of seconds later. The funny thing was, Pixie was just sitting on the sand as if nothing had happened to her.

"All she said was 'it was too hot in the clubrooms ... I couldn't stand it'. Lou then gave her a hand up and helped clean the sand off her dress. Pixie seemed okay. It was a relief to hear her speak normally again." Tracey let out a sigh probably wishing Pixie had spoken to her that way earlier.

"Lou got angry with her for going off without letting her know — the selfish bitch."

Tracey's eyes never left the bay as she continued in a whisper.

"Pixie didn't seem to remember anything about us talking. I was glad about that."

I placed my hand gently on Tracey's shoulder, not believing how unfairly she had been treated at times.

"Kane said he went looking for her earlier and couldn't find her — the lying prick ... After a few minutes, Pixie said she was fine and wanted to go home. On the way home, Lou and Kane basically ignored me, and each other, but we all wanted to make sure she got home safe. Pixie was laughing and talking at the start, then just after Joe's she started slurring her words and collapsed around the corner from the hairdresser's."

I rubbed Tracey's shoulder before letting my hand fall away and then said.

"And that's where I come in."

Tracey turned to face me and appeared relieved that she didn't have to explain any more.

"Michael, I can accept that not everyone in the neighbourhood likes me. But I hope you can understand that my parents were only being protective of me after New Year and shouldn't be hated for that."

Tracey's mood then seemed to change, to harden before my eyes; determination replaced sadness on her face.

"Well, I'd better get back home now. Dad wants me to help him straighten the side fence — how funny's that?" Tracey then said quickly, "Thanks for the chat."

I returned Tracey's smile and thanked her before she turned on her heels and left by the small overgrown path that would return her to the carpark where this terrible incident began.

My mind continued to race as I tried to rationalise my actions, as well as those of Kane and Lou, and how we weren't *there* when Pixie needed us.

Only Tracey was.

Then, I noticed a colour; a colour rarely seen in nature. It stood out against the dark green of the melaleuca bush. I stepped closer to the bush, leant down and then grabbed a few threads of what appeared to be cotton hanging from a splintered branch which protruded from the melaleuca's fringe. I stretched out the threads and then held them up to the sky.

Royal blue.

4

An emptiness accompanied me as I retraced my route past the Sailing Club and began to take on the steepness of the access road. I then noticed on the large stormwater drain directly below the old boat ramp, two teenage girls singing and dancing as they balanced on the curved surface.

The closest was Pixie, beside her, Lou. A beat-box sitting precariously above the outlet pumped out a *Spice Girls'* hit; a small stream of water trickled from the drain onto the sand and then snaked its way to the foreshore.

Pixie saw me and waved before pointing me out to Lou, who continued to concentrate on her dance routine. It was only when Pixie moved to jump off the pipe that Lou stopped dancing and grabbed her by the arm, preventing her from leaving. I wasn't exactly sure what that was about, but things between Lou and I would probably never be the same after I lost a large degree of control in her presence at the hospital.

Pixie then spoke to her, while pointing roughly in my direction. Seconds later Pixie worked her way over a sand dune pushed up against the path and then stood in front of me, immediately placing her hands on her hips.

"Hi, Michael. Tracey your bestie now?" Pixie said sarcastically. "Aren't you a touch old for her tastes?"

Pixie knew I wasn't impressed with her sarcastic remarks and before she could add her usual, 'Sorry ... only joking.' I stated, "Tracey's a good person, Pixie." whether she liked the comment or not.

"She's just learning to be comfortable in her own skin ... As we all are."

Pixie looked away from me annoyed before she said. "No, you're right ... Just give me a little time to remember it."

Pixie, then smiled as she changed the direction of our conversation by saying.

"I'm glad I caught up with you. I just wanted to tell you that Zac and I *are* happy that you and Mum are meeting this afternoon and maybe starting to get back together, or something — I'm serious ... Lou, Zac, and I are going out with my dad as well — somewhere."

Pixie then gave me the warmest smile. I wasn't sure of the reason.

"You know, I've finally realised, I can't blame myself

for what happened. It was entirely those guys' fault. They started this shit … No-one else." Pixie said.

"Somehow, I must have met them before … I know I wouldn't have taken a drink from people I wasn't sure of.

"That's the way I see it, Pixie, but I also know that I should have made sure you got home safe."

"Seventeen-year-olds don't need chaperones any more, Michael."

Pixie and I then stood in silence, a silence that would normally be uncomfortable, but instead was calm and easy, without the need to force a conversation; perhaps we had, without realising it, finally accepted each other.

"I've been doing a few different things lately." Pixie said, without giving me any indication of what.

I waited and then thought I should ask. "What sort of different things?"

"Well, I have a boyfriend for a start … Well, sort of a boyfriend."

"That's good. Does your mum know about this sort of a boyfriend?"

"No — and I don't really know him." Pixie said screwing up her cheek.

"That's different," I replied to her evasive answer.

"I just call him Horse Guy, because he's never told me his name — so that's what he gets."

"Horse Guy, hey? … Got a long face?" I grinned.

"Don't be silly, Michael," Pixie said as if she now owned the maturity high ground.

"I ran into him on Mordialloc Beach when I was avoiding Tracey a few weeks ago. She was walking straight at me on the bush path, so I went onto the sand and saw this guy trying to ride his Appaloosa into rough surf ... He was so infuriating this guy, but in the end, it brought back a lot of good memories of doing horse trails with Mum and Dad — I bet you never knew Mum was a real natural on a horse."

"She's never mentioned she likes riding to me."

"She loves it ... Well, she used to love it before she went all crazy about films — Anyway, I was so pissed-off when I saw this guy trying to make his horse do stupid things that I told him to get off."

"Get off — That's a big call, asking someone to get off their horse, just because you don't like the way they're riding."

"I know, but he was such an amateur." Pixie scoffed. "Although, it felt great to pat and be close to a horse again. When I used to ride, every worry, every stupid thing in this world would disappear; except for the horse beneath me and the wind in my face.

"Did he actually get off the horse?"

"No, he did not," Pixie said, a bit disgruntled. "He said one of the head trainers at Epsom wants his horse to learn to swim in the surf so he can put on condition. He said he would know more than me."

He might.

"Anyway, I watched the way this guy rubbed Brawler's nose and patted his mane, I could tell he would do the right thing by her. I said if we can get her to follow another horse through the shallows that would be a start. He's bringing Brawler down to Mordialloc Beach, next Wednesday afternoon ... so we'll give it a try then."

'We'll give it a try.' — Who's horse is it?

I could hear the volume on the beat-box being turned up and it was obvious what Lou was trying to do — Stop Pixie talking to me.

"Lou's so clingy at the moment." Pixie said in an exasperated way. "It's annoying the shit out of me."

Pixie swung around to look at the stormwater drain as the music from the beat-box cut to silence. Lou then picked up the box and walked steadily towards us.

~

"C'mon, Pix, we gotta go. Your mate Whalesey's getting dropped off about now with a guy who wants to join the club — He might be hot." Lou shouted as she came to a sudden stop in front of us, instantly grabbing Pixie by the arm and rudely trying to drag her away.

"I don't want to look too sweaty when they arrive."

"Sounds like you've been given the wingman's job," I said to Pixie as she was being towed away.

"Not with Whalesey — He's old news. Remember the party I had at home," Pixie yelled as her voice faded in the distance.

"I think he likes me *too* much."

I walked slowly up the steep steps beside the fresh-water shower, across the carpark and then stopped at the pedestrian crossing on Beach Road. I pushed the large round button, but I wasn't going to meet Fiona — quite yet.

~

5

She shouldn't have asked for more than I could give.

Pixie with her head bowed tried everything to rid her mind of Tracey and the time when they were friends. The beach ahead was Pixie's alone, and she thanked the God she no longer believed in for that. Waves broke and spread in random patterns, each trying to reach further inland on the wide tract of hard sand on which she walked.

Over her shoulder, the rising sun formed a silhouette of houses and scrub; its rays barely touching the sand. A cool onshore breeze picked up as Pixie reached the open expanse of Mordialloc Beach where ti-tree and mela-leuca thin.

The wind was strong enough now to whip Pixie's ponytail over her shoulder and rest it over the G on the windcheater her mother had brought her back from the

States, two years earlier. It was her favourite; snug and comforting, and she would never throw it away.

I'm getting too old for a ponytail… I'm not a kid anymore.

That's it, no more ponytails, pigtails, or any of the kind after I finish this school term.

I'll go to Rokk Ebony and get a bob, maybe even shorter, just like Tracey has now.

Pixie stopped to face the breeze and then looked out onto the bay, annoyed at herself for again thinking of Tracey, and for associating her in any way with being cool. No matter how hard she tried to stop them, two memories kept returning to her from New Year's Eve: one was a sense of falling, which she did not understand; the other a voice unclear.

'Pixie is that you? … Are you alright?'

Pixie held her breath, suddenly realising who had spoken those words and then recalled Tracey being thrown heavily onto the ground.

Tracey had tried to help me New Year's Eve.

She closed her eyes as a small eddy swirled up and around her, causing sand to sting her face.

I kissed her as a treat, I told myself then … a treat for whom? We swam together the same day I overheard my parents use the word 'separation' for the first time — only two years ago — I started this.

I knew Tracey wanted me, her open mouth and hungry tongue told me. I wanted it as well. I smoothed her thick mousy hair as she pressed gently into me. I cried the moment I came.

Tears ran down Pixie's face and flew off her cheeks as she continued to look out at the white-caps rising then disappearing in the middle of the bay. Suddenly aware she was no longer alone, Pixie looked behind her through scrub above the beach for anyone who wanted to steal the solitude she had searched for and found, and desperately wanted to retain.

On the small cliff to her right, customers moved like a blur around the Parkdale Beach Café. Pixie, then, out of the periphery on her left, noticed and then took a better look at a young man in blue Bermuda shorts and a black sleeve-less tee-shirt, sitting astride a wide-eyed Appaloosa, barely fifty metres away; urging it with stirrup and rein, to enter a bay churning with breaking waves and whipped by a strengthening wind.

What is that nitwit doing? Pixie thought while shaking her head. *He has no bloody idea.*

"Hey!" Pixie yelled as she swung around and made large strides over sand and surf to reach an oblivious young man and his immovable mount, which she judged reasonable in its refusal to enter the turbulent water.

"What the hell are you trying to do to that poor horse?" Pixie shouted as she reached to within a metre of the horse's right flank; overflowing with an anger that she couldn't believe was hers.

"You can't get a horse into the water by rubbing its tummy and throwing the reins over its head like a *Punch and Judy* show."

Pixie placed her hands on her hips in the usual fall-back position she had employed time and time again and waited for some acknowledgement of her advice. The rider whispered in the horse's ear and then smoothed its mane, appearing to not pay any attention to the meddler on his right.

"Get off!" Pixie screamed.

The young rider turned his head slowly and then looked down on Pixie.

"Beg your pardon?"

"You heard me ... If you don't know what you're doin' with friggin horses, you should get off their fuckin' backs."

The young man looked up and down the beach and then towards the carpark.

"Is this Candid Camera or something, or is your boyfriend in the carpark breaking into my float and four-wheel-drive? ... Or should I say my dad's."

Pixie thought about it for a second then responded sharply.

"No ... and no ... and thought so."

Pixie filled her lungs with the fresh bay air, felt the taste and sting of salt before breathing it out slowly; still wanting to scream at the young man, so smug, as he continued to gaze at her in wonderment. She also wanted to race home and hug her mum and never return to the beach she used to love so much.

"She's a stubborn bugger of a horse." The young man said, staring at and speaking to the water at the same time. "I was told if I can get her to swim in the bay, the battles over. I can do anything with her."

"Who told you that bullshit?"

"One of the head trainers at Epsom."

"He's taking the piss out of you, buddy." Pixie said and then pointed at the foreshore. "Can't you see the white strip of bubbles as the waves break — Horses hate that, they can't see what they're stepping into."

"If you can't trust a head trainer, who can you trust?" The young man returned.

Pixie wondered whether there was any merit in continuing a conversation with someone who doesn't even have a basic knowledge of horse training.

"Was she dumped?" Pixie asked turning back to face the rider, who continued to pat the horse's neck as it raised and lowered in a sign of agitation.

"A couple of months ago at my folk's property on the Peninsula. My parents are friends with Vic, a head train-er at Epsom, so…"

"Are you a stable hand?"

"God, no. I'm a painter. I just finished my apprentice-ship a year ago. Vic said as long as I paint a few stables … and rocks. I could have an old stall at Epsom."

"So you don't know what you're doing, with …?"

"Brawler. I named her that because I was given the stall of a fairly successful racehorse from yesteryear, called *Not a Brawler* … I was told she had an attitude — Just like someone else I won't mention."

"So, I was right. You're a try-hard."

"You're a try-hard. My folks owned purebreds for years. I was encouraged to ride the ones I could."

"You sound like a home-schooled hack."

"You can go now young lady and thanks for your kind advice." The rider said and then gave a forced smile as he tightened the reins to move his horse away.

"Take her back to Epsom and come back when it's still down here," Pixie said as she stepped over and began to pat Brawler on the neck. "She's in reasonable condition for a rescue horse."

"Yeah, my folks thought she must have broken out of her owner's paddock during a storm. They put up notices in the local papers and around Main Ridge and the Peninsula — but nothing … My folks didn't really want her, they were out of horses by then — So I said I'd work something out."

Pixie continued to pat Brawler on the neck.

"Listen, it's simple. Horses will follow another confident horse." Pixie said in a self-assured manner. "See if you can get Vic to bring down one of his horses which is used to swimming. Brawler looks smart, she'll follow it in. If you think that's the answer to everything."

"You're pretty damn sure of yourself, aren't you?" The young man said with a reluctant grin.

"I should be. I started riding when I was seven. I grew up either sailing in the bay or riding trails ... before my mum thought it was more important to make films than spend time with her family — and my dad got too busy drinking with his mates and playing around with whoever."

Pixie studied the open beach that ran towards Mordialloc Pier.

"We could try a slow walk through the edge of the shallows down there. She might respond. If I had some chaff, she'd probably follow me home."

With a dumb guy on her back.

Pixie let out a tiny giggle. The first in a while.

~

6

Saturday, 22nd February 1997. Afternoon

Truly Scrumptious was our favourite café, Fiona and mine when we were first courting; cosy and intimate, and not one of the cafes in Mentone where Fiona's friends gathered. It allowed us time to get to know each other without any undue pressure.

At short notice, Ceci, the owner, would reserve for us the small window table at the far end of the dining room, where we would sit holding hands like teenagers and discuss our future. A future which included my moving into Fiona's home and how it would be managed without any major disruption to the lives of her children.

I'm glad Fiona chose it as the place she wanted us to meet. It is perhaps the only place that might settle my nerves enough to discuss the giant impasse the words 'that includes you' threw up on the last occasion I was in her home.

Fiona was sitting at the window table, her eyes focused somewhere between the footpath and the large pot-plants in Granary Lane. She smiled and I wondered at what.

"Go on through, Michael," The barista said through a bearded smile and then added in his prominent Middle-Eastern accent. "Your flat-whites are nearly ready … Still no sugar?"

What the hell's his name? I thought while nodding my head and saying 'No, still good without it, thanks mate', before proceeding towards the dining area and my destiny.

I cautiously stepped up the small ramp and then in the direction of Fiona who continued to stare into space — I took her being off-guard as a good sign.

"What are you thinking about?" I asked as I arrived at our special table, declining to be too personal and include 'Fee.'

Without a start, Fiona moved quickly to stand, a smile still planted on her face.

"Hi, Michael," Fiona said leaning over to butterfly-kiss me on the cheek. "I was on horseback again — Sit beside me."

I sat diagonally opposite her at the table, close enough without being presumptuous. I continued the theme.

"I just had a dream that two flat-whites were being made by our favourite barista." I leant in close again and whispered. "Whose name I can never remember."

"Me either," Fiona said quietly back, our faces close, our eyes locked on each other's, then we both went silent and moved back a suitable distance, perhaps starting off too comfortable with each other, before resolving anything.

"I think Pixie's got a friend," Fiona said with a glow on her face which she didn't have the last time I saw her, taking our conversation in a direction that I didn't expect. "A male friend. How exciting is that?"

"Very exciting," I said and had to be careful not to give away too soon that I knew more, "Is he a local and do we have a name?"

"Now, those are things I do not know. All I know is that I happened to come across them as I was, you can't say stalking your own daughter — Let's say, making sure one of your children was safe near the water." Fiona touched my hand unconsciously and then continued on with enthusiasm.

"Pix and this young man, who was on an Appaloosa and looked quite alright from a distance, were yelling at each other. He seemed to be holding his ground against whatever Pix was throwing at him. Yet, they still went off together; him in the saddle, her on foot leading the way — That's where the horse comes in." Fiona concluded. I nodded in agreement but had better confess.

"Actually, I ran into Pixie down the beach, shortly before I came here. It was good to see her."

I hesitated. Fiona wouldn't enjoy that I knew something important about Pixie — before her.

"She did mention something about a horse guy."

"Oh, that's good … She looks well, doesn't she?" Fiona said, surprised and mildly taken aback with what I knew.

"She does look well," I replied as our coffees arrived on a silver tray carried by a young waitress with an expressive and familiar face. Also on the tray was a plate with a large vanilla slice cut into two. She removed each item carefully and placed them on the table in front of us.

"Hi, Haley," I said to a girl who had looked after our every need with a smile each time Fiona and I had met here.

"Thanks, Haley," Fiona said and then asked. "Now, did my office give you the schedule and flight details for Sydney? I'll kick their butts if they haven't. At the moment we're looking to keep your time slots down to four days?"

It then occurred to me that Haley was not only our favourite waitress but also acting in Fiona's new film. A film that will take Fiona away again, when her children need her here.

Now, that was an infantile thought.

Fiona continued, "You won't be getting into any trouble by taking time off, will you Haley?"

"No, Ceci thinks it's super cool to have an actress on staff. She's so excited to see how it turns out — So am I

— I'll be there with bells on, Mrs Farnes." Haley said, her face beaming as she gave both Fiona and me a tiny wave as she headed off to attend to the next table.

"Isn't she such a sweet girl?" Fiona whispered, "Huge potential to become a serious actress. Such a great cameo she did on my last TV pilot, not long before we met. I had to have her on-board for my new project."

I nodded again and then picked up and took a greedy bite from the piece of vanilla slice closest to me; icing sugar dripping off my top lip.

"Yum!" I said after finishing the bite, grabbing a serviette and wiping my mouth.

"You know the kids at the Girls' don't call vanilla slices, snot blocks any more… They call them *mille-feuilles*."

Fiona shook her head. "Bit pretentious." then asked in a more serious tone.

"How are your folks?"

"Pretty good." I said not ready to be torn away from our easy conversation, "Not exactly happy to have their forty-one-year-old son back in his old room."

Fiona could tell I was peeved, so she added in an apologetic tone, "I never intended things to go that way."

"How's young Zac?" I asked, still unable to forget the stunned look on his face when I was asked to leave him and his mother alone, almost two months ago.

"I miss him." I said and then was quick to add, "Don't ever tell him that."

"I won't and he's good ... Pix and Zac are good."

From the flat tone in Fiona's voice, I knew she was holding something back.

"Well, sort of good." Fiona eventually added. "I won't lie, things were difficult after you left. Pixie has had reoccurring dizziness, which is extremely concerning, but the doctors from the Alfred tell me to give it time. They've also both had counselling sessions set up by *SECASA*. Can't fault how good they've been for their self-esteem. The staff are so caring but tough when they need to be."

"Zac and Pixie are the most important things in this," I said and then saw Fiona's expression change from worry to mild disappointment.

"Aren't *we* important?" Fiona shot back, leaning forward on her chair to face me.

"Of course we are." I replied, "Just sometimes, parents need to take a back seat and give their kids priority."

"Are you suggesting that I haven't given my kids priority?" Fiona said, agitation growing in her demeanour.

"No, Fee, it's..." I then realised. "I'm not a parent, so perhaps I shouldn't say anything."

"Perhaps, you shouldn't," Fiona concluded bluntly.

We returned to sip our coffees, not unhappy, in a way, to use this circuit breaker to re-gather our thoughts and prepare for our next attempt at reconciliation. Fiona spoke first.

6

"Andy's taking Pix, Zac and Lou to the Lolly Jar Café sometime this afternoon. It's good of him to be more involved with the kids."

"They'll enjoy that," I responded without actually believing his company could be that fulfilling.

"I've asked Andy if he could come around more often to see the kids. You know, more support — He's been good, so far, cleaned up his act a lot. Surprisingly, Pix is not as over the moon to see him as I expected." Fiona said and then continued her momentum.

"It's actually nice to see *a* face around the neighbourhood," Her expression turning a tad gloomy.

"I haven't seen Roz and Jerry for weeks. Who knows how our friendship is — probably shot. I've only seen Steve and Jill a couple of times since I've been back. They're all about the Sailing Club being pissed off with the police attention it's been getting. And as far as Trev and Georgie are concerned. They might as well have dropped off the face of the earth."

Fiona then dwelled over her coffee before finishing it.

"And I'm heading north again in two weeks to start filming. Although, one positive. Pix and Zac are coming with me for as long as their schools will allow. Which I think is pretty fluid."

Fiona had finished her coffee but not her vanilla slice. I eyed it off.

"Wait and see how I go first Michael," Fiona said knowing me too well. I then asked.

"Have you heard anything from the cops?"

"Actually, Detective Clarke called me two days ago, to say they'd questioned a couple of blokes sleeping in a white panel van in a carpark at Parkdale Beach. Both guys had bleached hair. They found a small amount of grass in their van, but neither of them was called Michael."

"Perhaps, Michael was never a real name."

"Most likely." Fiona accepted before continuing, "The two guys said they were both down the Peninsula at a party on New Year's Eve. They said they had witnesses."

"How convenient for them," I said with a tinge of bitterness.

"Detective Clarke did also say her office received a call from a young man who wanted to remain anonymous, saying he had information about New Year's Eve, then just hung up," Fiona said as she pushed her vanilla slice towards me.

"Interesting..." I stated, but in reality, pissed off that this guy couldn't muster up enough courage at the end of a line to do the right thing.

"...he might call back." I added.

Fiona then unexpectedly grabbed my hand under the table.

"What are we gonna do, Michael?" Fiona asked, squeezing my hand, her eyes searching my every gesture to see if I was really interested in fixing the damage done to our relationship.

"I don't know, Fee. Asking me to leave with Roz and Jerry that day, hurt me more than you could ever believe."

"I know that now, Michael. I wasn't thinking straight. I had to be alone with Zac. You can understand that, can't you?" Fiona said, her eyes moist with tears.

"I wanted our relationship to be perfect." She continued. "It *was* perfect until I went away."

"There was no reason for that to change. Throughout this, I have done what I thought was necessary — and right. Nothing could have prepared us for the night we had. I tell myself I acted responsibly ... Obviously, I didn't."

Fiona let go of my hand.

"I can understand in a way why you would mention Pix and Tracey had ... been together. People can get jealous and possessive and I do feel responsible for not concentrating more on my kids, but I also hate seeing Tracey in so much trouble. It wasn't all her doing — No wonder she turns her back on me when I see her walking."

"Fee, Detective Clarke asked me straight out if I knew of any relationships Pixie had had in the past — I wished I'd never answered."

Fiona seemed to accept what I had to say and then chose her following words carefully.

"One thing I'll never understand and it had *nothing*

to do with what happened on New Year's Eve, but why did you have to tell the police that you caught Zac and Tracey together?"

I looked deeply into Fiona's eyes with an expression of disbelief, incredulous at what I'd heard.

"Fee," I whispered, "I didn't say anything to the police about Tracey and Zac … you never gave me a chance to tell you."

"You never gave me a chance."

Fiona's face showed her shock. She reached down and found my hand.

"I'm sorry, Michael. I'm so sorry. I thought it had to be you — Oh, my God, I'm sorry."

Fiona then lifted my hand and kissed it, her tears wetting my fingers. She leant her face in close to mine.

"During my marriage, Andy would keep things from me — which I hated. It was easy to find out what they were, though. But, he was rarely — present. Deep down, I knew he was a single man reluctantly wearing a ring — I accepted that."

"I have a thing about secrets."

Fiona kissed me on the lips, neither of us concerned that nearby tables, in fact, all the tables, were now aware that an important moment was playing out.

"Michael, I'm dying every night I can't be with you. I do love you and I know it will take time for us to get back to anywhere near normal." Fiona said squeezing my hands.

"Please, I want you to come back home ... Pix and Zac want you back as well ... They understand you couldn't have done any more than you did. Can you please give me, and my family, another chance?"

I wanted to put Fiona and myself out of our misery and say I would come back, but something large was getting in my way — Pride.

"I love you, Fee, and that hasn't changed, but how can I after what was said."

Fiona then poked her tongue out at me, completely out of kilter with my statement.

"You're really pissing me off, Michael. I didn't want to but seeing you're getting all antsy about this. I'll have to bribe you."

"Will you now?" I grinned, happy to shed some gloom.

"Yes, I will," Fiona said, accepting that I was now on her wavelength and wanting just like me to get past this stalemate.

"Yesterday, I got a call from the Chauvel Cinema in Sydney. They were confirming their theatre for the premiere of *The Money Trail* in September — Cross everyone's fingers."

Fiona batted her eyelids. "Please do me the honour of accompanying me on that night. It would mean the world to me."

I shrugged my shoulders as if not interested.

"Film premieres — Never thought they'd be that interesting."

Fiona pressed her lips hard against mine, then moved them back and said with emphasis.

"Perhaps, if you went to one, you would find out they are."

I was proud of Fiona for making me see sense. It was time I stopped the fight and surrendered to the inevitable.

"Are Pix and Zac going?" I added only because I wanted them there.

"They're going," Fiona replied.

"In that case, I'd be honoured to accompany you, Ms Fiona Farnes."

I didn't want to ruin this by saying any more. I stood, still holding Fiona's hand.

"Come on, I'll walk you home." I said and then added, "If you don't mind, not past the Lolly Jar Café."

Fiona stood and then wrapped her arms around me to an enthusiastic round of applause from the occupants of the dining room. We both turned and showed our appreciation with a small bow.

I whispered in Fiona's ear,

"We'd better go."

~

7

Saturday, 15th March 1997. Morning

From my sun-drenched location in Fiona's courtyard, I could hear from the bottom of the side path the click of the pool security gate as it released from its coupling.

I couldn't see who had opened it, and it didn't matter; they would have to come past me to get into the backyard and with a decent amount of anger still left in my gut over what two disgusting young men had done to Pixie, and Tracey — I would dare anyone to try.

A light crunch on stones and soon the intruder was looking around the corner of the house while carrying a bulging plastic Myer bag; the bright red collar of a woollen jumper poking out of the top.

"Oh!" Roz said stopping abruptly by a possum ravaged weeping-rose.

"Hi, Michael … I didn't know you were back." Roz looked back down the path and then to me again.

"Well, I am," I replied, as coldly as she deserved after the contempt she had shown to me in this house two and a half months ago.

"Look, I was just dropping this off to Fee. I don't like leaving things out the front, just in case they're taken." Roz over-explained while showing me the bag I could already see,

"It's a jumper that'll fit Zac. Jerry says it's as warm as toast, but the colours are not him — Such a fashionista."

"Leave it with me, Roz. I'll pass it on to Fee when she gets back." I said a tad friendlier, petulance not a good look for a grown man.

"Fee's at Southland with the kids. Shouldn't be long, if you'd like to wait. I've just made some coffee — Plenty in the plunger."

Roz walked over and placed the large Myer bag on the table in front of me, and then turned to leave.

"No, I'll catch up with Fee, later. Thanks for the offer, though." Roz said at least politely before adding. "See ya."

Roz took two steps towards the path and then stopped, held her stance for an excessive amount of time, before spinning on the spot and delivering a bewildering statement.

"Have you," Her peaches and cream complexion now rosy in the late morning sun. "Got half a brain?"

Roz then paused, white knuckles now on her clenched fists.

"Have you any — bloody — idea what you've done?"

I was right! You're a serious piece of work, Roz.

"If you have something more to say, Roz. You should say it — I've got time." I stated calmly in response. "No use bottling it up."

"No, I don't think I can. I'm too bloody angry."

If Roz wanted to leave, she could. Her need to say more was keeping her here.

"How do you take your coffee?" I persisted.

Roz bit her lip and with her eyes squarely on mine, walked over and stood before the outdoor setting.

"Long black — No sugar, thanks." Roz finally got out.

Don't dare say 'I'm sweet enough'.

"Grab a chair. I won't be long."

I left for the kitchen without a shred of concern that Roz wouldn't be there when I got back — Too much had been left unsaid when we were both asked to leave this house.

~

When I returned with the long black, Roz was seated forward on her chair, opposite mine on the corner of the long wooden table; her arms crossed — ready to go into battle.

Roz went on the offensive as soon as I had placed the long black down.

"Wasn't it bad enough, Pixie being attacked, without

bringing up details of what our children had done? It would have been so embarrassing for Trace, Pix, and Zac at the start, let alone what the real damage will be in the future."

I accepted Roz's outburst, without highlighting her ignorance by pointing out that it wasn't me who had told the police about Tracey and Zac or had mentioned *anything* in detail.

"Once these sort of things are out — They're out." Roz continued, struggling with her emotions. "You can't control the hurt. If good parents find out early enough, they can protect their kids, and then lay down the law, if they think it's necessary."

"This has poisoned the neighbourhood and damaged many friendships, Michael — and it didn't have to happen!"

I took my time, had a slow drink of my coffee and then responded.

"I think you're being a bit unfair on me, Roz. I was overwhelmed New Year's Eve — You were there, you know how bad it was."

"No, I don't think I'm being too harsh on you. You have no idea of the state, Fee, Pixie, and Zac were in after Andy walked out on them … I'm so pissed off I had to see them that way again."

Roz picked up her coffee, had a sip and then seethed with a new wave of anger.

"You know, a lot of people think that Fee has *the* perfect life, rolling in money, the jet-setting lifestyle of a movie producer to go along with it ... Well, that's bullshit! Andy took half the money and gave fuck-all back to the kids; and if you haven't already been told, this friggin' house is mortgaged to the hilt to finance *The Money Trail*."

"I have no idea of Fee's finances, Roz ... It's not my business."

Roz withdrew into herself briefly before continuing.

"I know these things because Fee used to confide in me about everything, including how happy she was to have found love again."

Roz held back tears as she said.

"And now it breaks my heart that we're no longer friends."

Roz closed her eyes, lowered her head and again tried to control her emotions. Seconds later she sat back and wiped her eyes.

"I'd better go." Roz said calmly as if a massive weight had already been lifted off her shoulders and then went to stand, "If you could pass the jumper on to Fee that would be great."

"Roz, can I please just say something before you go."

Roz was reluctant but again settled on her chair.

"Of course." She said quietly.

"Before I moved into this house, into this

neighbourhood, and met you and Fee's other friends, my life had become so insular — by my own making. Basically, I had given up. I didn't think I could be around people again. I was then asked to go to this and go to that and before I knew it I was feeling comfortable around people again. I do appreciate your part in that Roz. I did the wrong thing by Trace and I do apologise to you and Jerry for that — with all my heart."

Roz sat staring at me. She wanted to punish me more but knew I couldn't have been more honest.

"Thanks for saying that, Michael. I *was* being hard on you before, it stops me from blaming myself." Roz said with a degree of relief in her voice and then added.

"As a mother, you think you know your daughter … Obviously, I didn't. If I had given Trace, a tenth of the time I gave Fee's family, I would have known what her feelings were. Not to say that I could have done anything about them." Roz then produced the beginnings of a smile.

"I do remember what I was like as a teenager — Nobody could stop me from doing what I wanted."

With Roz more receptive, I wanted to show her that I had tried to rectify some of the damage.

"I'm not sure if you're aware of it or not," I said, "but I have spoken to Tracey a couple of times along the beach over the last few months, and have gotten to know her reasonably well in that time. I have come to realise how courageous a young woman she is ... and as are both, Pix, and Lou."

"If the three of them could be friends, life would be a lot easier." I added, "But you know that's unlikely."

"I know and it may be hard to believe, but Trace and Pix were inseparable years ago. Unfortunately, a couple of years back, they stopped talking to each other — just like that. Fee and I tried to find out what was going on and get them back together, but they shut us out completely."

Roz and my ears then pricked up as we heard the garage roller-door engage and rise. Roz with a hint of panic stood and then pushed her chair back in.

"I'm going this time, Michael. I hope Zac likes the jumper." Roz said with unnecessary haste.

"Don't you want to say hello to Fee and the kids first?" I asked, feeling she must want to.

"I can come back another time ... just not now."

Roz did want to stay and talk to Fiona. That's why she came here. I had to somehow convince her of that.

"A week ago, I was standing in the exact same spot as you, listening to Fee go on and on about wanting to drop in and say hello to *you*, but she was unsure how she would be received after the way things had been left."

"That's silly. Our door is always open — even to you, Michael."

"Thanks, but don't you see, it's the same as you leaving now when you have a chance to sort this out."

Fiona's face then peered through venetian blinds stretched wide open, she looked at me and then Roz. Seconds later, footsteps could be heard striking the polished floorboards of the family room as they increased in pace; double doors flung open and soon Fiona was running around from the back of the house into the courtyard.

Roz turned and then took hurried steps towards the side path.

"Where are you going, Roz?" Fiona shouted in dismay.

"I've got to get back home, Fee — I have to go."

From the end of the outdoor setting Fiona took off, running with determination she pushed aside chairs until finally catching Roz in a strong embrace at the entrance to the side path.

"You're not going anywhere, Roz — I mean it — until we talk about this." Fiona cried out as she turned Roz around and took her into her arms, "Okay?"

Roz managed to nod her acceptance as Fiona pressed her cheek tightly against her friend's.

I knew Fiona and Roz would want to talk privately, and as they were no longer aware of my presence, I discretely left the courtyard to return to the house.

In the family room, I could see Pixie peering through the venetian blinds, watching intently the proceedings in the courtyard.

"They should have done this weeks ago." Pixie said

turning to face me with a heightened enthusiasm for the new development.

"Quick, come and have a look. They're holding hands now and sitting down to talk."

"They *need* to be friends," Pixie added firmly.

I leant in beside Pixie to see her mum and Roz deep in conversation. Their fight was over. Perhaps it was time for another fight to end.

"They do need to be friends," I agreed but had to say more.

"Don't you think it's about time that you and Tracey were friends again?"

Pixie glared at me with a look that said *none of your business,* but it lacked the anger and dismissiveness to make me think that it wouldn't be considered.

There may be hope.

I felt a light tap on my shoulder as Zac pushed in close beside us to have a look outside.

"How's it going out there, old fella?" he asked in his usual laid-back style.

"See for yourself," I said letting Zac shuffle in next to his sister.

"I think it's gonna be alright."

The End

An Extract from
Sebastian Carmichael

I could hear my destination, well before I saw it. Intermittent yelling, booing and even roars of laughter grew louder and louder, the further I went down Coventry Street. I turned right onto a large block of open land, shocked to see well over a thousand people moving around the dusty expanse. A bright light on the fascia of a hall lit up a roughly-built podium, ten yards in front.

How was it possible to entice this many people, so far out of the way?

I slowly mingled through the crowd, taking only sideways glances at the mixed bag of hard-faced men and occasional rough-looking woman that formed the majority; only a sprinkling of well-dressed types and people my own age were game enough to venture into this company. The rumbling storm clouds overhead gave the whole scene an unnatural feel, creating the impression that it was close to dark, when there had to be at least another hour of daylight left.

The focus of the crowd quickly shifted towards the makeshift podium, where a tall skinny man was striding confidently towards a rostrum, hastily lifted into position by two burly men. The skinny man wore a thick shapeless brown jacket, completely inappropriate for the heat at present, and sported a salt-and-pepper beard that came to a point in front of his green tartan tie, giving him more the appearance of an aristocrat, than the dungaree clad type I expected to front a crowd like this.

The glaring light behind the rostrum also gave the man the unexpected allure of a fire and brimstone preacher, ready to bring the wrath of God down on the unfaithful below.

The crowd roared with laughter as insults began being hurled by several rowdy groups, unwilling to wait for the speaker to commence before taking up their sport. A lot of these same blokes poured beer down their throats and then swore with a crudeness that would make wharfies blush.

"Shut up you morons! Listen to what I have to say," the thin man yelled in a broad Scottish accent.

"This country has been bled dry by greedy bloody bosses for too long. They have no respect for what the average worker does for them. They want to send us to an early grave, while they count their profits. We need to unite, to stand up to the capitalists. And we need to do it *now*!" his voice rose to near breaking point.

"Ya look like ya never worked a day in ya bloody life, ya scrawny, pansy bastard," shouted a thickset bloke wearing an army slouch hat, his mates giving him huge pats on the back as they took long swigs from their beer bottles.

This was great!

I moved a little closer to the front.

"I will have you know that I was wounded on the Western Front in 1918, and how much compensation did I get?... *Nothing*!" the skinny man yelled again, stretching out his arms like he'd been crucified.

"I got shot in the Dardanelles, mate," another old digger shouted.

"That hurts more!" The crowd roared as the large man in the slouch hat held his crutch, digging up an old joke he knew would be a winner.

"I think he's right!" protested a young man standing behind me, silencing the loud-mouths for a second, everybody nearby taking a step back to reveal the audacious upstart.

Well! If it wasn't the angry young man from the Aid for Spain stand, without his girlfriend, Elaine, to keep him in line. He strode to within five yards of the big-mouthed interjector, pointing to the platform.

"Why don't you get up there and tell us your great plan,

King Kong, instead of hiding behind your drunken mates ... Well, imbecile?"

"You'd better be careful what you say, you smart little shit. We were fighting the Hun when you were still sucking on your mother," the Digger shouted in response, his mates moving as one towards the over-confident young man.

The thin man on the podium, who everyone had temporarily forgotten about, threw in his two bobs' worth in a vain attempt to save the smart-arse. "What the young man is trying to say is that ..." he searched for the right words, "the government can change things to suit themselves. They can send you to a government doctor, and they'll stitch you up for good."

A lot of people in the crowd nodded in agreement, but I didn't think it would be enough to stop this young bloke getting a hiding he would never forget.

"The trouble with you old army rejects is, you were fighting the wrong enemy. Your commanders were puppets of their capitalist overlords, who profited from the death and misery of your mates," mocked the Aid for Spain worker, holding his ground as the large Anzac ran at him, his face as red as a beetroot.

I moved forward myself, to try and help this smart-aleck, for no other reasons than to return a favour and minimise the pummelling he was going to get from the rampaging bull almost on him, but I was blocked by a surging mass desperate to see some blood flow.

Through the bobbing heads of a crowd at fever pitch, many of whom had swiftly taken sides, I could make out two large figures which stepped beside and then ahead of the young man.

"*Whoa!*" the crowd groaned as a huge blow was landed on the army veteran, just before he reached his objective. The king hit delivered by a massive assailant made blood spray from the Digger's mouth as he fell back into his mate's arms, who then managed to prop him up against the woodwork of the podium. I stood mouth agape, not only at the ease of the victory, but by the fact that there were two pugilists of equally humungous size. These two near identical twins stood either side of the unflinching antagonist, their arms crossed like the boxers you might find in front of a take-on-all-comers tent at a country show, waiting to beat up a local cocky.

I thought this little kerfuffle would have satisfied the bloodlust of the crowd, but the mood only got uglier as scuffles broke out in every quarter. I decided this place was too hot for me, and it might be better to make a dignified exit without any further ado. When more mates of the Digger turned up, and started to throw bottles in the direction of the twins and their handler, I moved right out to the periphery.

Just then, a woman's shrill voice eclipsed all others. "Gun!"

Everybody froze on the spot, eyes darting all around,

trying to locate the person who could put them into the next world. No-one was sure what to do next; someone needed to take the lead.

Bang!

A loud clap of thunder cracked from directly above, making me and everyone else around me jump out of our collective skins.

I knew running wasn't the right thing to do, and something I promised myself never to do again, but I ran as fast as I could back into the shadows of Coventry Street and then as far away from the Red Square as my legs would carry me, only slowing to a walk once I had crossed over the Yarra at the Spencer Street Bridge.

An Extract from
The Beautiful Journey

Hitting a rut as he tried to turn into our camp, Denny and his bike fell into a dusty heap, the only thing left to see was an arm holding a bloodied rabbit high in the air.

A second later, Denny jumped to his feet and declared "I brought supper."

⁓

"Make us a bit of room for me bunny on the plate will ya, girls?" Denny asked, after he had, in front of everyone, pulled the guts out of, peeled the fur from, and then dressed flat the unlucky rabbit that had wandered across his path as he flew into Zumsteins.

"No! — ya not putting any myxo-ridden roadkill, anywhere near this hotplate, Danny," Janet yelled as he approached the plate. Jude and Lindsey then stood back from their filling of a tin tray with charcoaled meat.

"It's Denny, and ya got plenty of room on the right … so, cut us a bit of fat from a chop and rub it over the spot, will ya, sweetie?"

"I said, NO! — Denny, or whoever you are?" Janet replied, hands on hips "Ya can't just wander into our camp and take over."

"It's alright, Janet," Lindsey threw in, a little embarrassed by her attitude "We're finished with the plate."

Janet ignored Lindsey and then turned her back on everyone, scraping down the hotplate to emphasise that no more food was to go on.

"Denny's always welcome, where I'm campin'," I shouted to Janet, then shortly afterwards the other blokes joined in, calling Denny to come over and cook the rabbit on the open fire, stuck through one of our makeshift metal pokers.

"How'd ya know we were here, Denny?" Roy asked on helping him push the rabbit onto a blackened rod.

"I ran into ya mate, Greg, earlier today. He's a bit of a toss that boy, but he reckons he was coming out to Zummies, tomorrow, and said you'd probably be hidin' out behind the kangaroo paddock — payin' nothin' for the site."

"Greg'd know about payin' nothin'." Roy laughed.

—

After Denny had knocked down a few of our Fosters cans, and then bullshitted on at length about his recent, amazing, and sometimes hairy trip through central Victoria and up into New South Wales, he then, without warning, stood up and strode over to his motorbike, which was still lying abandoned at the same spot where he had crashed it.

Out of one pannier bag, he pulled two bottles; one wine shaped, the other beer. After standing the bike up, he pulled from the opposite, squashed pannier bag, a long metal tube, which he then took the cap off and drew out what looked like a scroll.

"I got a treat for every one of you bastards — and bitches," Denny declared on carrying his booty back to the camp fire, where all, except Janet, had gathered to keep warm from a cold nip that had crept into the clean mountain air.

"I came across a hermit living in the hills at the back of Kyneton a few weeks ago, on my way back from my trip up north. He said he had worked out how to bubble marijuana smoke through his home brewed beer."

"Whoa!" Roy yelled out "Crack one open, Denny."

"I'm not touchin' it!" Janet declared from just outside the communal tent, before having a long swig from her bottle of Cold Duck wine.

Denny ignored Janet and said that the hermit wanted to help everyone achieve the highest clarity and fulfilment in their lives, and he believed that was possible by using a combination of several swigs of his home brew, waiting a half an hour, and then reading a passage from his book, *The Beautiful Journey*, which corresponded to their place in life's journey.

"Sounds like the hermit's spent too much time in the bottling room, Denny," I joked, with no support from the rest of the crew, who were beginning to show quite an interest in Denny's story.

"Let's go then, Denny," I shouted "I'm ready for enlightenment."

With oily disheveled hair falling over his dusty face, Denny, raised his arms to the cloudless sky.

"I'm going to read a passage that the hermit chose for me, which I think could apply to all here, it's called *The Lady beside the Murrumbidgee*."

"So, let's get drinkin'!"

—

Half an hour later, I found myself lying sideways, my head held up by a tuft of grass, looking at the group who had joined Denny's experiment: all blokes. Occasionally, I could see the faces of the girls bobbing about in the vicinity of the main tent.

Denny pushed all the blokes back to one side of the glowing fire, then sat cross-legged, and began to scroll out the parchment paper. After a long pause, Denny broke his silence.

"In the year of our Lord, nineteen hundred and sixty-eight, I found myself on the banks of the swollen Murrumbidgee River. It was the first Sunday following the Paschal full moon."

"That's like now," one of the girls whispered "Easter."

"I became spellbound by the natural beauty of the river, the life-blood of the Wiradjuri nation, as it flowed with new vigour after recent mountain rains.

Reluctantly, I moved to continue my journey of discovery, when I noticed a billow of red fabric beside a river gum on the near bank. It was a young white woman, seated with her back pressed hard against the gum, a bustle under her now rested skirt.

I turned to step away from this young lady, to leave her in peace, when she cried.

'I am not afraid. Do not leave the tranquillity of the river because of my presence.'

I then asked if I may sit beside her as company, to which she agreed. I tried to look away, but noticed her right arm, unseen, vigorously motioning at the place of her sex."

"Hey!" Rod yelled, and then went quiet.

"'Would you prefer that I leave you to your pleasure, young lady?' I asked as gently as possible, to which she replied.

'I am in the twentieth year of my life, and as yet, cannot achieve the total release of pleasure and spirit, to permit the lover of my choice, to reach deep within my body.'

'Perhaps for me, as with many other women, this may remain a mystery.' The woman then held her breath as her back arched.

'Alas, I am determined not to leave the river today, without trying to reach this place with myself alone.'"

"This is SICK!" Janet yelled out, a slur in her voice. A chorus of shushing followed.

Denny continued.

"I was moved by her plight, and pondered what to do to aid this woman.

'Have your lover's been kind?' I asked

'They have. The men have been gentle with their members and tongues, women with their fine fingers. But, I am still left wanting.'"

"Stop this shit — Right now, Denny boy," Janet screamed out.

"Women are not filthy like that."

Enz, nearing his limit, called out over his head "Just let Denny finish, Janet … you might learn something."

Denny continued.

"'Pardon, young lady, but I am no different to any other man, so I cannot help you. But, if you would grant me one selfishness before I leave. I would be most grateful.'

'Certainly, young man, but you may not touch my sex.'

I asked if I may watch her search for pleasure, to which she agreed, and then slowly began to draw up her red skirt with her left hand, to reveal her right hand, continuing to thrust deep and hard, and then suddenly rub above in a small circular motion."

"Tell him to stop, Roy ... Peter ..." Janet almost begging for someone to listen.

"As the evening sun's rays were released from a cloud, they left a golden glow on the young woman's legs that immediately mesmerised me. I asked, without expectation, if I could kiss them. To which, I was surprised, she agreed.

I knelt down, but smelt no pleasure as I kissed her left thigh. As I moved to the right, I felt her hips rise and spread, then smelt her sweet perfume in my nostrils, as I kissed the other.'

'Continue.' she demanded."

Janet raced over and ripped the parchment from Denny's hand, tearing it up in front of his face, before throwing the rod and shredded pieces onto the low fire.

Denny, with rage in his eyes, rushed over to Janet, grabbed her by the arm, and then dragged her forcefully to the edge of the campsite, before letting her go.

"Go to where my kit is and get ready for me." Denny ordered.

"I'm not going with a fucking animal like you." Janet yelled at Denny through tears, losing all composure.

"GO!" Denny screamed into her face, pointing to the far side of the track.

Janet searched the camp, her eyes pleading for someone to stand up for her — until realising — after a terrible silence — that no-one was going to come forward — nodded her head, turned slowly, and then walked to the other side of the track, where she was soon out of sight.

Denny followed shortly afterward.

Nobody moved an inch, or spoke a word.

Acknowledgements

I am so grateful to have had the support of so many wonderful people in the production of *The Moonbeamers*.

Sincere thanks go to my editor Deb Seeary for her love, intuitive editing, and unwavering support during the writing of the book, to Chris Mitchell for his amazing image of two teens on Seagull Rock; the cornerstone of the book. To Sarah for allowing the beautiful words of Chris Wilson to be a highlight.

Many thanks also to Wendy for her knowledge and love of horses which shone through on the page, as well as to Courtney Nottage, Amy Seeary and John Seeary for their insights into the complex world of the medical and teaching professions.

A deep gratitude goes to the bayside community around Mentone for giving me the inspiration to write this book, this includes Colleen and the crew from Truly Scrumptious, who allowed a crucial part of the book to be set in their iconic café; and not the least to Gerard for being the heart and soul of the Mentone Hotel.

Once again, I am indebted to Luke Harris for his vision and professionalism in the design of this and my other books.